The guards' walkie that there was a problem

Outside the electron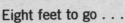 away van was now in Sy_____ _____ __ sight. She willed herself toward it.

Eight feet to go . . .

Five feet . . .

Then suddenly Nikolav called out, "Excuse me. . . . Excuse me. Stop!"

Sydney ignored him and closed the remaining gap to the exit doors. She knew Nikolav had to operate the master release button at his podium. *Please Vaughn, stay still. Let me spin whatever plays out!* Sydney fought the urge in her to pull her weapon and blast her way out. Instead, she turned her head back to Nikolav, her left hand sliding under the gurney.

A lump of doubt settled in the back of her throat.

Also available from

SIMON SPOTLIGHT ENTERTAINMENT

ALIAS™

THE

apo™
SERIES

TWO OF A KIND?

ALIAS™

THE

SERIES

FAINA

ALIAS™

THE apo™ SERIES

FAINA

RUDY GABORNO AND CHRIS HOLLIER

An original novel based on the
hit TV series created by J. J. Abrams

SSE

SIMON SPOTLIGHT ENTERTAINMENT

New York   London   Toronto   Sydney

S|S|E

SIMON SPOTLIGHT ENTERTAINMENT
An imprint of Simon & Schuster
1230 Avenue of the Americas, New York, New York 10020
Text and cover art copyright © 2005 by Touchstone Television
All rights reserved, including the right of reproduction in whole or in part in any form.
SIMON SPOTLIGHT ENTERTAINMENT and related logo are trademarks of Simon & Schuster, Inc.
Manufactured in the United States of America
10 9 8 7 6 5 4 3 2
Library of Congress Control Number 2004115765
ISBN 1-4169-0245-7

To Big Rudy, for giving me the courage to try.

For Green Eyes

CHAPTER 1

PRAGUE

After the collapse of the Warsaw Pact, many of the major cities of the former Soviet bloc toppled under the weight of their top-heavy bureaucracies. The obsolescence of their industrial centers left them susceptible to the growing pains that come with revolutionizing a people and its government.

But Prague was the exception.

The city experienced a rebirth after the ponderous yoke of the Socialist state was lifted, and it rapidly became the envy of Eastern and Western Europe alike. Artists, intellectuals, and the populace in general exploded in newfound freedom.

With the celebration of cultural and fiscal self-sufficiency came the economic powers, who were more than ready to use the city as an example of the birth of the new Europe.

Along the banks of the river Vltava, on the Bubenské nábrezí, stood a district known simply as "the riverfront." This was a place where the rich and powerful made their homes. Here were houses whose lavishness would cause the city's former leaders to roll over in their graves. Uppermost among the extravagances was privacy. And those who dwelt there guarded their tranquility as only those with great affluence could.

Not all of these buildings were owned by the captains of industry or robber barons of the new Europe. Instead, some estates were unofficial consulates of the economic powers of the West. They were places that allowed governments secure locales to do things better left unseen. Everything from the nuclear disarmament pact to the fabric of national currency rates was brokered from the buildings in this district. The destruction of documents from the time of Stalin through last week's Middle East diplomacy took place here.

FAINA

The three-story stone house with etched glass windows at 372 Vinoteka Street was such a place, and it was maintained by the Russian Federation.

"You just don't understand!"

"Well, why don't you try and explain it to me."

"You wouldn't get it. You *never* get things when it comes to me!"

She regretted saying it even before the last word came out of her mouth. The silence between them now was painful, and the hurt she saw in her mother's eyes didn't help the teenage girl's resolve. She wanted to be seen as an adult, yet her mother's crossed arms were a nonverbal statement that she still needed guidance.

Both were too tired, and too stubborn, to fend off an argument that had grown excessively familiar. The daughter recognized their standard battle cries, but it was her mother who decided not to play out their archetypal roles this time.

"You'd better go to bed. Tomorrow's a school day."

Before either could say anything else, her mother turned to leave the room. Both of them wanted to say something more, but the time had passed for that. No new ground was being broken in their conflict. There was nothing left to do but separate their viewpoints with a heavy oak door.

Her mother left without making eye contact. It felt like the forced calms between rounds at a boxing match. A great deal of unfinished business was left to sort out.

Dropping onto her bed, the young girl stared at the ceiling. Her flashing green eyes were the only indicator of the frustrated anger and guilt that consumed her. It was this combination of teenage angst and culpability for wounding her mother's feelings that made her so irritable. *It's killing me to be expected to act like an adult, and not be treated like one.* Faina Sorokin couldn't wrap her thoughts around it. *Why do I have to be what they want me to be?* Running her hands through her brown hair, she continued to stare at the ceiling.

The filtered goggles gave everything in the room a distinctive reddish cast, but they were necessary to ensure his night vision. At first he thought, as he peered through the window, that she looked younger than the seventeen years her file indicated. He patiently waited out the argument with her mother. He couldn't understand what she was saying, but it didn't matter. She was a teenager. Whatever the language, it was always the same thing.

Moving in silence, the man left the window and made his way along the mansion wall. Covered from head to toe in black tactical gear, he was virtually invisible. Even in the full moon, his stealth suit helped to make him a fixture of the shadows. Moving slowly, deliberately, he reached the service door at the rear of the kitchen. Through an adjacent window, he saw a woman in her mid-twenties. She was dressed in a maid's uniform. Slowly, and without a sound, he pulled out his knife. . . .

The first floor of the house had many rooms designed for both comfort and display, yet only one was a favorite of the current occupants. The study had been converted into a lush office filled with Old World antiques and dark mahogany paneling. But tonight it seemed to envelop the man deep in thought at his desk.

He was a reserved gentleman of average height and build, and although he was no longer young, as evidenced by the smattering of gray in his hair, his physique still retained the athletic build that he had maintained since college. His face was distinguished, and when it wasn't focused on the myriad of political documents, it commanded what his wife often referred to as "a certain schoolboy charm."

In the fireplace, the smoldering embers cast an ever-dimming glow, painting Anton Sorokin in hues of soft orange. He tried to keep focused on yet another petroleum production report. *God, will this never end?* His eyes drifted, as they often did, to the painting hanging above the mantle. A near-perfect copy of Gauguin's *Spirit of the Dead Watching*.

It was given to him by an old college friend in the Bonn office of Interpol. "I know how you are about paintings, Anton," his friend had said when he handed him the brown paper–wrapped painting. At first Sorokin was hesitant about taking the undeniably exquisite gift, but his friend assured him, "Don't worry, the man who painted it won't be needing it. By the time he gets out of prison, he won't be able to lift it, much less sell it."

Sorokin had to admit that not much persuasion had been needed for him to accept the gift. He was mesmerized by it. The texture of the paint, contrasting with the simplicity of the subject matter, often reminded him of his job—both straightforward and complex at the same time. Maybe that was why he liked it so much. All he knew was that it had followed him from post to post for more than a decade now, always ending up in his study, undoubtedly at the suggestion of his wife. He smiled at the thought of her. Just by looking at his face, she could tell his every thought, every feeling. "It takes you away from this," she had told him once. "And better a painted girl than a *real* one," she often teased.

"Ogling your little girl again?" His wife's voice caught him off guard.

"Guilty as charged."

"Why don't you come to bed? Whatever's so important can wait until morning."

He sighed. "Then I'll be even further behind."

Sorokin watched as his wife, Anna, walked into the center of the room. *Even after all this time she's the most beautiful thing I've ever seen.*

She was tall and slender. The past thirty years hadn't aged her as much as distilled her, like a fine bottle of wine or a good Italian opera. Sorokin stood and walked over to Anna, his partner of twenty-five years. Seeing the look on his face, a knowing smile crossed hers. She placed her head on his chest as she nestled herself in his arms, breathing in the comfort she always found there.

He recalled what a sharp contrast she had been to his work. It never ceased to amaze him how lucky he was to have her. She always knew exactly what to do. She kept him centered. Before big speeches she'd send him two bars of Andre's Swiss chocolate. That was his favorite and she never forgot. She'd listen to his arguments, never letting him get away with anything so that he was always prepared.

Above all, she kept him from being consumed by the machine of the political economy. So many of their peers had gotten lost down that road, consuming themselves only with world issues and leaving family and marriage behind. "No work talk today," she'd say, and take his hand in hers. "Today you're all mine."

Sorokin watched his wife as she moved around the study straightening things—at this hour it was a sure sign that she was anxious.

"Did you two quarrel again?" he asked. Anna was not the only one who could read the nuances of the person she loved.

"Of course. . . ."

"We knew this was going to happen sooner or later."

"I know. It's just . . . I didn't think it would be quite this difficult," she said. "I can't seem to say anything to her."

Sorokin held her, comforted her.

"If she were a boy, it would be me, you know."

Anna pulled her head away from his chest and looked up at him, a wry smile on her lips. "You could have mentioned that to me seventeen years ago."

He held her closer, loving her more than he thought possible for someone he had known so long. He smiled, knowing he took a little of her pain away.

"What was I thinking?" he joked.

The maid's body lay in the rear pantry. He had dispatched her quickly and quietly, carefully wiping his blade on her apron when he finished.

The agreed-upon language was English, and he spoke it into his throat mic. "Four secured."

The tinny voice in his ear replied, "Roger Four. Begin your sweep."

The man moved with catlike stealth. The security agent at the monitor console never had a chance. The knife slid between the agent's forth and fifth ribs, piercing his lungs. Pushing the body aside, the man scanned the bank of monitors in front of him. What he saw pleased him. *Everything is moving like clockwork. The rest of the team accomplished their tasks.* Then he found his target. Quietly speaking into the mic, he alerted the others. "They're in the study."

He looked down at his forearm and the small map in its laminated sleeve. *Time to earn my wage.*

Sorokin still had his arms around his wife.

"Well, I'm going to bed," she said.

She lifted her face to his and they kissed once. And for a moment Sorokin stopped thinking about petroleum futures.

When she pulled back, Sorokin could still sense her tension. "I'll talk to Faina in the morning," he offered.

"No, this is between a mother and her daughter. I'll do it." Anna stepped out of his arms and smoothed the front of his shirt. "Come to bed soon," she said.

"I will," he promised.

She kissed him once more, this time with a little more behind it. It was warm and everything the papers on his desk weren't. Pulling away, Anna sighed, and without another word, turned and walked out of the room. Sorokin watched her body move away from him. He turned and found his political papers mocking him from the desk. It was a delicate balance, the life he had chosen, but the brief exchange with his wife reminded him exactly why he worked intently on the issues of the world.

Faina sat on the edge of her bed, still analyzing her conversation with her mother. *Why does she have to be that way? It wasn't even a real tattoo.*

She decided to occupy her mind with other things.

Faina looked over at her computer. She still had to deal with the moron in that chat room before she went to bed. Sitting in front of the terminal, she logged in and began typing her reply. She had been present (virtually) at a lecture given by an American nanotechnician two nights before at Argyle Hall. *How could an MIT professor be so totally wrong in his assumptions about microelectrical feedback in nanocircuitry?* She was relatively confident that she was going to bury him tonight.

Damn it, she thought, as her mind drifted back

to the conversation with her mother. Her best friend, Paula, was going to give her a really hard time about her tattoo being gone. They had promised to keep them until Friday to wear them to a party. "Your mom's going to lose it when she sees that," Paula had predicted, and she was right. Faina had hoped to talk her mother out of making her remove it. But in the end, Faina was convinced that her mother considered the mark symbolic of her refusal to act responsibly. As soon as her mother voiced that opinion, Faina knew it was over. That was always the crux of their fights.

Great, school is going to suck tomorrow.

The hallways in the building's residential section were carpeted, which made it much easier to move quietly. The intruder had confirmed that his target was in the back bedroom, and there she was, working on the computer. Quickly and silently he began to move in. . . .

Anna stood at the base of the stairway, listening to the house. It was as quiet as it always was this time of night, save for when her husband craved a late-night snack if he was working late, which was too often. But now it was serene. *I guess that's why I like it so much,* she thought. *It gives you time to think, to reflect on things you didn't have time to think about during the day.* These quiet times were cherished in the life that she and Anton had chosen.

"If only she were a boy," Anna murmured, and smiled to herself. Her husband was right. She loved her daughter immensely, but she had to concede that sometimes—and just sometimes—if she had known how hard this was going to be, she might have had second thoughts. The feeling stemmed greatly from the realization that she and her daughter were so similar. Both were curious, intelligent, and headstrong.

About to head up the stairs, Anna stopped. *What is that?* It was small and almost invisible in the shadows at the end of the hallway. *A rat? No, surely not in this house.*

Anna walked down the hallway toward what she thought she saw. Thinking about it for a moment, she pulled off a slipper—just in case she were to come upon one of those vile creatures.

Then a sound!

Not loud. Like the floor giving after the shifting of weight. For a moment she considered calling Anton, but she immediately dismissed the thought. *I've been a helpless mother already tonight. I don't need to be a helpless wife, too.* Besides, she knew there was a light switch just around the corner.

Anna reached carefully for the switch, her silk weapon at the ready in her other hand. Her fingers hit what should have been the light switch, what should have been hard, cool plastic. When she felt the object she touched instead, she couldn't initially define it. It was . . . soft, smooth, but hard underneath . . . leather! But before she could think another thought, two gloved hands grabbed her and pulled her into the darkness.

Sorokin looked across the room to the reports open on his desk. Sighing, he gave the painting one last glance and walked back to his work. Just as he reached his desk a voice startled him.

"It was always one of my favorites."

A man Anton Sorokin had never seen before was standing calmly in the center of the doorway, dressed completely in black. He seemed to melt into the shadows behind him. Beyond surprised, Sorokin could only watch as the man entered the study. His confusion only expanded once the stranger began to speak. The uninvited guest's eyes flicked up to the painting above the fireplace.

"I always admired its clarity," the stranger said. "Its message. It says, 'I like the beach and I lust after young girls.'"

The man walked over to the mantel, reached up, and gently ran his fingertips along the surface of the painting. Not moving from behind his desk, Sorokin put on his bravest face. He found himself holding a deep breath. He tried to surmise the nature of business of the man before him. *What is truly going on?*

"I think you've misinterpreted Gauguin," he said. "True, the painting is of a young native girl, but if you look past—"

"Nonsense."

The mystery man spoke the word curtly, but kept his voice at an even level. "Academic tripe used by those unable to accept a simple, if unpalatable, idea from an artist."

The man in front of the mantel reluctantly took his eyes from the painting and faced Anton Sorokin. What Sorokin noticed first was that his eyes were the most piercing blue. They seemed to look right into his mind and read his thoughts. He hated the way this stare felt. It measured him. A faint, thin smile spread across the man's face. It didn't, Sorokin noted, reach his eyes.

"You disagree." The man didn't phrase his words as a question. "I find that most people are reluctant to believe the worst in anyone whom they have taken the trouble to put on a pedestal."

The man casually walked over to the desk. He glanced at the pile of reports spread across the work space. Sorokin was still unable to move.

"Although I will admit to you, I was expecting more from a man of your intellectual reputation."

At that moment another man, dressed in green tactical gear, came through the study doorway. He shot a glance toward Sorokin that sent an ice-cold chill down his spine. *Where is my family, and how many men are here?*

The man in black looked at his coconspirator. Noting Sorokin's lack of mobility, he smiled his empty grin and excused himself to the doorway.

Sorokin strained to hear what they were saying, but his attempts were in vain. The strangers spoke too low for him to hear. The second man, obviously a lieutenant, pulled out a small flip chart and indicated something to the man in black. The lieutenant did not look happy, and what little Sorokin could hear had a slightly apologetic cadence. When the man in black did finally issue orders, they were short, sharp sentences. Quickly the lieutenant left to carry out his instructions, leaving Sorokin alone again with the pair of icy blue eyes.

"Anton Sorokin, it is necessary for you to come with me right now, please."

"I'm not going anywhere with you—"

"Minister Sorokin. Perhaps I misspoke."

Almost on cue, the muffled sound of a struggle could be heard upstairs. For the first time, Sorokin became physically agitated. His eyes looked to the ceiling, to the noise, and then urgently he headed for the door. The intruder shifted slightly to block his advance.

"My family!" Sorokin cried.

"Is being loaded into our vehicles as we speak."

"Why?" Sorokin said, trying to regain control of the situation. "Where are you taking them? Who are you?"

The man in black walked back to the painting. He oozed control. They both stood there a minute, the intruder and the minister. When the man finally spoke, his matter-of-factness, not his words, chilled Sorokin to the bone.

"Do you know what it really is that I love about this painting?" the man asked calmly. He didn't wait for an answer. "Its conviction. I was always interested in Gauguin for this reason. He was an artist, an average *man,* with average dreams, though not without ambition. He had a wife and a family . . . and then one day he decided to leave it all. Just dropped everything and never looked back. Very much akin to a man shedding the shackles of conformity. How liberating that must have been . . ."

At that moment the lieutenant came back to the doorway to indicate that they were ready to leave. The man in black stopped him with an upraised finger. Once again he pierced Sorokin with his eyes.

"Don't you see? By freeing himself of the apparatus of society, he was able to pursue his vision . . . his art in its purest form. He was able to be true to his innermost self. And this was the result."

The man brought his lieutenant in with the slightest nod of his head. Working quickly, efficiently, he bound Sorokin's hands with plastic zip cuffs and then covered his head in a thick cloth sack. When the lieutenant finished, his superior leaned in so he could whisper parting words in Sorokin's ear.

"And as to your query about who I am, minister, I am like Gauguin . . . a humble artist searching for the truth in my work." The man seemed pleased with his words, and added, "But you may call me Victor."

CHAPTER 2

LOS ANGELES

Michael Vaughn was sweating. Hunched over the low table, he was the epitome of coiled tension. His brow was furrowed in concentration; he was obviously struggling with a difficult task. He manipulated the small pieces, trying to figure out which combination would yield the dividends he so desperately needed.

"You're not going to make it," Sydney said. Her eyes were locked onto his.

"Cut it out. I don't need any more pressure."

"Vaughn, seriously, time is not on your side here. Let me—"

"No, no. I got it. Are you ready?" he asked.

"And waiting."

"Here goes." Carefully he placed three more tiles in a row. Then Vaughn playfully spelled out his word. *T-A-X-E-S.*

Sydney stared at the tiles Vaughn just placed on the Scrabble board. With a sarcastically exaggerated look of disbelief on her face, she sat back in the sofa. "*Taxes*? I waited ten minutes for *taxes*?" she said.

"It's a word. And it was hardly ten minutes."

"I wouldn't bet on it if I were you," she said playfully, and in Vaughn's eyes, pretty cutely. She continued to rib him. "You understand this is not frat-boy, remedial Scrabble, but rather what I like to think of as the adult version of said game."

"First, I wasn't a frat boy, and second, I resent the idea that you aren't recognizing the beauty of my use of the *X*. It's worth, like, thirty points there."

Sydney laughed as she looked around her house. It was strange, but until very recently she had never really considered it home. It seemed to her more apt to think of it as somewhere to keep her things when she was at work. Watching Vaughn reach for new tiles and then remember that Sydney had drawn the last of them on her previous turn, it suddenly occurred to her that the place was becoming more than that. Considering what had befallen her previous apartment, and her life, she had good reasons to hold her emotions back. But she was trying to make a point of *letting herself enjoy life.*

And then it dawned on her. Her place by the beach didn't just seem more like home to her because she was getting used to being in it. It was becoming more to her because *he* was there. It was strange, because although it wasn't the same—how could it be, Michael had been married for God's sake—but having him there, *with her,* sort of made the whole notion of having a place . . . real.

Vaughn made a point of looking at the large clock hanging in the kitchen, and then took great amusement in toying with Sydney. "You ready to put your money where your mouth is?"

Sydney concentrated on her tiles. "The question is, are *you* ready?"

"Do your worst, Bristow." With that, Vaughn sat back on the couch, watching her.

Looking down at her options one last time, Sydney started laying tiles down almost immediately.

Vaughn watched, a little shocked at her speed, as each letter was placed around the *X* he was so proud of utilizing.

E-X-U-R-B-I-A. Vaughn was stunned. With the look of an angel, Sydney showed him that, yes, she had used all the tiles she had left.

"Exurbia?! That can't be a real word."

"I think the dictionary might beg to differ."

"Use it in a sentence."

Sydney thought about giving the actual definition of the word, but instead smiled and announced, "Exurbia. Vaughn does his *taxes* in exurbia." She fell back against the couch, laughing wildly.

Vaughn shook his head, and Sydney regained some semblance of composure. She picked up her wineglass and watched him flip through the dictionary. Seconds later the look of absolute defeat that came over his face told her he had found the word. He tossed the book on the love seat next to him and pushed deeper back into his own cushion. *This is perfect,* she thought. *The game, the quiet. Having Michael here and not a single worldwide threat in sight.*

"Hey," Vaughn said with a slight smile.

"Hey."

"What are you thinking about?"

"I don't know . . . nothing," Sydney said.

That was a lie.

"Us, maybe." She didn't mean to say that, but with the wine and the laughter . . .

Vaughn leaned forward and picked up his tile rack. "I couldn't find all the letters." He could see that she didn't understand what he was talking about, so he simply turned the rack around to her.

U-R-C-U-T-E.

Sydney looked at the rack and then into Michael's eyes. He dumped the tiles into the box, embarrassed at his grade-school suaveness. Setting her wineglass down, she leaned closer to him.

"Sydney," he said, "there's something that I've been wanting to say to you."

"What?" Sydney moved over to sit next to him on the love seat.

"It's been so screwed up lately, so really . . ." He searched for a way to share what had been going on inside him, but he couldn't find the right approach. He tried again. "It's been so messed up. And sometimes I feel like there's no way we're ever going to get back to where we were."

Sydney could see the pain in his eyes, and it made her want to hold him, keep him safe and warm until the pain went away. In a way, she already understood what Vaughn was trying so desperately to say. Part of her knew that she should help him, but the other part wasn't sure if *she* was ready for that yet. Instead, she listened.

"I just need you to know that whatever it takes, I'll do it," he said. "I just want for us to be . . ."

Sydney could feel herself melting. *This* is where she wanted to be . . . maybe.

"Be what, Michael?"

Vaughn moved his lips closer to hers. "What?"

Subconsciously, Sydney's lips began to move toward his. Then they both heard the sound of a key in the door. Moments later the front door opened, and Nadia Santos practically fell in, her arms overwhelmed with paper grocery bags.

"I can't believe it. The Argentine grocery stores here are better then they are back home. Sydney, you won't believe this. I saw this guy and he was so—Vaughn! What a surprise!"

The moment was lost. Vaughn and Sydney shared a brief glance, feeling like high school kids whose parents were home early. Vaughn sat up and began putting away the Scrabble board. Sydney stood up and rushed to the entryway to help her sister with the bags.

Nadia gave Sydney a questioning look, but Sydney ignored it. They put the bags on the counter in the kitchen.

Sydney eyed the many overflowing bags. "How many people did you buy for? Or are you telling me that we aren't eating enough?"

"I thought I'd cook us a real Argentine dinner . . . all seven courses," said Nadia.

"All this for two people?"

"I thought we could invite some company. . . . Vaughn, for example."

"Or Weiss, maybe?" It was Sydney's turn to give Nadia *the look*.

Nadia dismissed it as her sister had, and she began putting the groceries in the fridge.

Vaughn walked up, putting his jacket on. "Hey guys, I gotta go."

Nadia looked up from the groceries. "You can't. I just got here," she said with sincere disappointment.

Sydney sat on one of the bar stools. "That's right. You can't leave yet. You need to demonstrate your superior Scrabble skills for Nadia."

"I'm pretty good myself," Nadia quipped, "but we have to play in Spanish."

"Sorry, guys, but I'm supposed to meet—"

Suddenly Vaughn's text message alert went off on his cell phone. Seconds later so did Sydney's. Like dominoes falling, Nadia's followed. All three silently read their messages. Vaughn was the first one to speak.

"I'll drive."

Sydney, Vaughn, and Nadia walked down the converted electrical access tunnel toward the white light of the APO bull pen. Sydney always felt a little intimidated by the type of light they had down there. It was the one thing about APO that she still couldn't get used to. Even though the complex was a good thirty feet below the surface and encased by as much reinforced, lead-shielded concrete, it always felt like midafternoon inside. She had commented about this to Marshall Flinkman once, and he told her that a Rand Corporation study indicated that illuminating windowless rooms in this way, with light that mimicked not only natural light, but specifically the kind that occurred in the spring between the hours of three and five, resulted in fewer claustrophobic reactions from inhabitants, and actually increased productivity. For that reason, Arvin Sloane had insisted on having such a system installed during the renovation.

All Sydney knew was that whenever she spent long periods of time in the complex, she lost all sense of day and night. It felt like a casino, and ultimately both experiences of time stopping often left her wishing she had a small window to look out of.

A funny thing occurred to Sydney as she, Vaughn, and Nadia walked to Sloane's office. APO had a vibe different from the CIA, just as SD-6 had one different from the Rotunda. Unlike the Rotunda, though, APO was more casual, intimate. This was most noticeably reflected in the way the personnel dressed. Sure, part of it was cover; in the real world, they were all supposed to work for a bank, and business casual was in. But generally, because of the nature of the job, the way people dressed better reflected their personalities. Sloane's impenetrable ego could be seen in his impeccable attention to detail in his clothes.

But her father never changed. For as long as she'd known him, Jack Bristow had dressed the same way. It was as if the pristine white shirts and the perfectly tailored suits were a sort of armor that protected and distanced him from everything. Sydney was taken aback by the unexpected surge of sympathy that swelled up from deep inside her. How lonely that must be, not being able to trust anybody. But was it sympathy or empathy? The past five years had been hard on her, very hard. And she knew that many of the convictions she once had, about right and wrong and the very natures of good and evil, had changed or just faded away. But how much of her father did she see in herself? *I was different before.* She knew that. *But am I becoming my father now?*

As the trio entered Sloane's office they found that Dixon, Marshall, Jack, Weiss, and of course Arvin Sloane, were waiting for them.

Eric Weiss caught Nadia's eye and indicated the empty chair next to him. She smiled, but instead sat next to Marcus Dixon on a small sofa. Weiss looked crushed. Vaughn put his files down next to his friend and sat in the seat he had just offered Nadia.

Weiss leaned in. "Thanks, buddy. But I was hoping for a more attractive neighbor."

"This is work, not playtime," Vaughn retorted.

Weiss smiled across the room at Nadia, who stealthily returned the expression.

Wasting no time, Sloane picked up a remote and hit the switch to close the privacy doors. "Now that we are all here, I think we should begin." The lights in Sloane's office dimmed as the large monitor came to life. A series of images, obviously from surveillance cameras, filled the screen. Sloane handed a small bundle of folders to Marshall to pass out. "These are photographs of the Russian sterile house in Prague."

Looking up from the hard copies of the photos in his file, Dixon asked, "Sterile house?"

"A sterile house is an installation used by governments, unofficially, when politically delicate or sensitive work is being conducted," Jack answered.

"Like spying?" asked Sydney.

Jack smiled. "No. It's in the open. Its main function is to guarantee a level of security not available in the usual government complexes, like an embassy, let's say."

Sloane went on. "Lately the Russians have been using this particular house to prepare for the EU Energy Conference scheduled to take place in two days in Prague. Because of the sensitive nature of this meeting, APO has all the important participants under surveillance."

Weiss interjected, "We have a black-ops division babysitting an oil conference?"

Sloane responded in his usual even tone, which always gave Sydney the creeps. "Not all of the attending, only the five primary speakers. Energy, specifically oil, is a hotbed of international conflict these days. Other countries are looking for any excuse to ignite long-held grudges. The stakes here are unimaginably high, not only for Europe as a whole, but for the United States as well. We're not interested in the crude; we're interested in not sparking wars." With a look that nailed Weiss to the floor, Sloane sat down at his desk. "So although it *would* have been a good idea to have overt operations protect it, we deemed the situation much too volatile for an acknowledged government agency to have anything to do with it. So . . ."

Vaughn shifted in his chair. "So they called us."

"No," said Sloane. "Actually, I recommended our team. This is strictly a European affair. But since these conferences are crucial for maintaining stable petroleum reserves, and as I just illustrated, international harmony, it was decided that APO would maintain surveillance and monitor the situation. Our agent in the Russian house was Marie Zhorkov. Her cover was as a domestic. Her mission was only to observe and to notify us if anything was not running smoothly."

Sloane clicked the remote and a new image flashed onto half the screen. It was of a still from a surveillance camera, showing a young woman in a maid's uniform lying prone in a kitchen pantry, positioned in the center of a pool of blood. The second half of the screen filled with an APO identification photo of the same woman. Sydney couldn't help but notice that the woman looked just a bit younger than she herself was. She and Nadia exchanged looks, both thinking, *This just as easily could have been one of us.*

Sydney looked over at Sloane. "And I guess things haven't been smooth, or we wouldn't be here. Right?"

Sloane gave a curt nod and then continued. "Six hours ago, a group of men from an ultraconservative neo-Soviet terrorist group broke into the house and kidnapped a Russian delegate and his family. Our agent was eliminated during the assault, as was the rest of the household staff. You'll find the transcripts of Zhorkov's last few weeks of transmissions in your files. Agents on scene were able to secure these images from the house's security system. The terrorists took all the bodies with them. The house was left spotless. Very professional."

Sloane clicked the remote again, and passport photos of Sorokin, his wife, Anna, and their daughter, Faina, replaced the images of the dead agent.

"This is Anton Sorokin, senior minister of natural resources for the Russian Federation, and his family. Sorokin's wife, Anna, is a minor diplomat with the ministry of finance and of no consequence to these meetings. Faina, their daughter, will enroll early at MIT next year."

Dixon asked, "If they wanted to undermine the conference, I understand the minister, but why take his family?"

"That's one of the things we'll have to find out."

Jack chimed in. "Collateral?"

Sloane's response was short and uncertain. "Perhaps."

Paging through the folder, Dixon asked, "What do we know about the kidnappers?"

"Not much. I hope to have a better idea soon."

Sydney and Dixon exchanged a look. Whenever Sloane made that kind of cryptic suggestion about his private sources, it reminded Sydney that her boss was still in many ways a man operating off the radar. Furthermore, it recalled the mandate that came directly from Hayden Chase: *Keep an eye on Arvin Sloane.*

"All I can tell you now is that the leader of the group is most likely this man." The photos on the monitor were replaced by a fuzzy image, taken from video, of a man wearing a black suit. "His name is Victor Pushov. He was a high-ranking officer in the KGB before the fall."

Nadia asked, "What is the Russians' official position on this?"

Sloane sighed. "Quite frankly, it's not very good. They are threatening to pull out of the conference and are accusing the other participants of invalidating them, arguing that they were attempting to undermine Russian's rise to dominance in the European petro market. They've speculated that numerous countries could be responsible, but they haven't ruled out Pushov working on his own. Our president has persuaded his Russian counterpart to delay any accusation for forty-eight hours, which is the day the conference is slated to begin. They have agreed to keep the whole thing under wraps until then. That is how much time we have."

Vaughn closed his folder. "To do what?"

"Minister Sorokin's importance to the summit is that he was to provide information on future Russian petroleum production. Because of the dire condition of the Russian economy, we must get him back before the meeting, or it could cause the total collapse of the Russian economy and perhaps that of the entire region. And Sorokin has to be returned before anyone knows he's missing. There are powerful forces, both in Russia and out, not to mention other industrial powers, that would like nothing better than to see this conference fail— and many will use *any* excuse to condemn it."

Sloane sat down behind his desk and picked up four mission packets.

"Intel indicates that Victor is most likely using some of his old espionage network in Prague. The fact that he had to dispose of numerous bodies in a hurry points to this building." He hit the remote again and the image on the monitor switched to two: On one side was a surveillance photo of a mortuary, and on the other side was a graphic of the building's floor plan. "Sydney and Vaughn will infiltrate Victor's safe house while Dixon overrides any security protocols he can from the outside. Nadia and Marshall will compile as much intel on Victor and his group as possible and continue to monitor the situation with the Russians," Sloane said.

The look he gave Nadia expressed that he was aware of her disappointment at being kept on the sidelines, but he chose not to address it. "It's crucial that we find out what Victor has in mind. If we don't, stopping him may only postpone the catastrophe."

Sloane went on. "So, we have to recover Anton Sorokin, and his family if possible, and return them without anyone knowing, before his speech. It is imperative that Sorokin be at that conference and imperative that no one knows he was taken."

Sloane turned off the monitor, and the lights came up. The doors to his office opened; the briefing was over. Nadia left immediately. As the rest of the team filed out, Sydney found herself face-to-face with Sloane.

"Sydney, may I speak to you for a moment?" he asked.

This was never a good thing for Sydney to hear,

but she didn't really have a choice. Just the thought that he was her superior again made her skin crawl. It was too much like the old days at SD-6. For a brief instant she felt like she hadn't accomplished anything in the past six years. Eyeing Sloane, she was reminded of Satan bargaining with Faustus.

"I was wondering if I could speak to you about something that's not job related," Sloane said, not even pretending it was a question.

Sydney's look said no, but she didn't leave, so Sloane pushed on. "It's about my daughter."

"I really don't have anything to say to you without her being here," Sydney said.

"I just wanted to say thank you for letting her stay with you."

Sydney didn't say anything. Sloane pressed further. "I asked her to stay with me, but of course she declined. I'm sure you can guess why."

"We've never really talked about that."

"No, of course not. And I would never ask you to. It's just that I'm afraid that she needs someone to talk to. She's alone here. A lot has happened to her in the past few months, and I was hoping she would confide in me, but that doesn't look like it's going to happen."

Sydney couldn't believe what she was hearing. "So you want me to recommend that she have open dialogue with you about your not being around when she was a child? Not seeing her even though you knew she existed, and letting her live in an orphanage, *alone*? Is that what you want me to say to her?"

"I was hoping you could relate to her what it was like growing up with a man like your father."

The remark made Sydney livid, and for an instant her eyes acquired a scary look that Sloane had only seen in Jack Bristow. It said, *I hate the man before me*.

"Look, I don't deal with my father," Sydney coolly replied. "I don't talk to him. I don't have dinner with him. I don't even like him. Outside of this place, I don't interact with him in any way."

Sydney stepped closer to Sloane in order to convey the rage bubbling inside her without announcing it to the whole office. Her voice was now both low and intense. This, too, reminded Sloane of Jack at his most intimidating. "But as bad as he is, and he is *bad*," Sydney continued, seething, "he can't hold a candle to you."

She turned and walked out of Sloane's office.

Just before closing the door behind her, she turned and said, "If Nadia doesn't want anything to do with you, I applaud her decision, and there's not a chance in hell that I'd try to change her mind."

The first thing you lose, Sorokin decided, looking around the room with no windows, *is your sense of time. How long have I been in here?* he thought. *A few hours? Days?* The plain cinder block walls gave him no hints about his current location. The tiny window in the door was equally unhelpful—he couldn't determine anything other than the fact that the wall across from the door was made of the same cinder blocks.

Anna! Faina! Are you here also? Don't worry! I will find you! Sorokin resisted the urge to throw himself against the door, to try to claw his way out. He knew emotional outbursts meant nothing to men like Victor. He had known colleagues who had met with the undesirables of the world. His own experience told him that bottom-feeders never strive to please their captives, and the victims who protest don't make it out alive.

At first he had been shocked by the whole ordeal. But as it began to sink in, it occurred to him that even his own country had only been out from under the oppressor's yoke for a short time. Sorokin had been thirteen when his father was taken to the gulag, not to be seen for years. It was his father who had taught him about men like Victor, men who only scoffed at what they referred to as "the weakness of nonbelievers."

This troubled him, and the desire to attack the door rose again. Trying to stay centered, he reminded himself that they must need him. He would be dead already if this was not the case. And as long as he was needed, he had at least a small chance of seeing his wife and child once again.

Turning from the door, he looked at the two pieces of furniture in the tiny room: a battered wooden table and an equally beat-up chair. When he was first shoved into the room, he had contemplated breaking the furniture in order to create some sort of makeshift weapon, but he had thought better of it. He'd decided, rather, that he should mentally lock himself into doing what he needed to do to maintain his family's safety. *Without them, nothing will matter.*

A loud *clank* followed by the sound of a bolt turning in the door jarred Sorokin back to the dangers at hand. As the cell door slowly creaked open, he tried to prepare himself for the mental agility needed to deal with his oppressor. Before Sorokin could move, Victor's presence filled the doorway. Nothing could hide the viciousness in the man's eyes. Sorokin decided to take the offensive.

"My family—"

"They are here, Minister," Victor said.

"I want to see them."

"Of course you do, and I would like to show them to you . . . later. Now is the time for you and me to talk. Please sit down."

Sorokin didn't move, and neither did Victor. Then a burly man, whom Sorokin remembered as one of the animals who had dragged him in here, appeared behind Victor. The man was thick and ominous, clearly the two talents for which he was hired.

Sorokin reluctantly dropped into the chair. The thug left the room only to return with another, much more comfortable–looking chair. He placed it across the table from Sorokin. Victor took his time to sit. Sorokin didn't bother hiding a bitter scowl. They both knew who held the power.

A tray with two glasses, a pitcher of cold tea,

and a small metal creamer boat was placed between the two men. Victor put a glass in front of Sorokin and began to pour. Filling the glass three-quarters full of tea, he filled the rest with milk, Muscovite-style.

"Anton . . . may I call you Anton?" Victor asked, never taking his eyes from the glass.

The minister said nothing. He was preparing his body for the beating, for the pain that he was sure would come.

Victor dropped a spoon into Sorokin's glass. Only then did he look up at Sorokin, offering his guest a dead-eyed smile. "I am a man with few trappings, and I will try and make our time together as pleasant as it can be."

"Victor, I would like to see my family now."

Victor grinned his empty smile again as he began to pour his own tea. "You will see them soon enough. I personally promise you that. But for now I think it is best that we all remain where we are." Victor took a sip from his glass. "I have a proposition for you. . . ."

CHAPTER 3

The C180's interior was austere at its best and a government-concocted torture device at its worst. Sydney and the rest of the team were dressed in army dungarees. They sat spread out in the three rows of lumpy passenger seats just behind the flight deck. The plane was loaded with cargo destined for Frankfurt. Once the aircraft landed, the team was to mix in with the ground crew and then make their way to hangar B-48, where a fully equipped van would be waiting for them.

Sydney winced as she shifted in her seat, trying

to find the least painful position to be in. She was a little annoyed at Jack and Dixon's convincing job of ignoring the bumpy ride as they read through the dossiers that Nadia and Marshall had delivered to each of them just before take-off, as if they were sitting casually at the local coffee joint on a Sunday morning. There was no doubt in her mind that they were forming a plan even now.

Part of her knew that she should join them. It's easier to improvise on a plan gone wrong if one knows its origins. But she couldn't deal with her father, or even Dixon, at the moment. Sitting in the plane on the way to the Czech Republic had given her time to think. When Vaughn opened up to her in her house, she should have been so happy. She had longed to hear him say he wanted to be with her ever since she called in to the CIA when she woke up in Hong Kong.

Sydney turned to the back of the cargo area. Behind the mountain of supplies destined for the base, Vaughn was going over the op-tech Marshall had provided for the mission one more time. He had always been thorough in his mission prep, but since Lauren Reed's death he seemed almost obsessed with it. Sydney resisted the urge to go back and talk to him. First of all, they were on a mission, which meant she had to keep her mind on the situation at hand. Second, she had no idea what to say to him. *We're not the same . . . but more important, I don't think* you're *the same, Michael. . . .* No. That was a bad idea, she decided.

But the thought was still titillating. *Was his promise real at the apartment?* She knew that Vaughn wanted to be with her. They had joked about marriage in the past the way that couples do when their feelings are more serious than they let on. She wanted to marry Vaughn, but time had been against them, and she worried. *If I rush this, if I believe him without proof, will he let me down?* Her thoughts circled through her mind. *I'm ready to have a relationship with the Vaughn I knew, but I'm not sure who he is right now. . . .*

It was too much to contemplate. Vaughn's honesty had touched her, but she decided to watch for his actions to mesh with his words, which, she admitted to herself, were quite nice to hear.

Trying to think about *anything* else, Sydney's eyes drifted over to her father, which reminded her of the conversation she'd had with Sloane. *I can't believe Sloane. The list of people whose lives he has ruined is massive. He didn't just make a few mistakes in his life. He sought people's destruction.* It sickened her, thinking of the metered smile on Sloane's face when he had compared himself to Sydney's father. *There was no way I would recommend that Nadia have anything to do with him.*

Sydney shook her head, trying to clear all personal thoughts from it. *Focus! Or there'll be nothing left of you but a dark spot on the road.*

But she couldn't. Everything she had said to Sloane was true. Sydney didn't like her father. In fact, what she felt for the man was very close to loathing. *But if that were completely true, why did I get so angry when Sloane tried to compare himself to him?* Her eyes again found Jack. She made a mental note to examine this when she had time.

"So what do they say?" Vaughn asked, dropping into the seat next to Sydney and snapping her out of her thoughts. She looked down at the dossier in her lap.

"Well, this Victor guy is a real piece of work. Ex-KGB, participated in a failed coup attempt against the old Soviet government in '91. After family connections got him out of prison, he disappeared and is thought be part of an ultrareactionary group that's trying to reinstate a strong central government."

Sydney flipped the page. "APO really did its homework on this guy. Marshall must have hacked into the Russian security network. This psych file is directly from KGB Internal Affairs. . . ."

Trailing off, Sydney read the file silently until Vaughn nudged her. "How about for those of us who don't read Russian," he said, grinning.

Sydney smiled at him. "Man, this guy's intelligence index is off the charts—with an unusually high amount of alpha wave activity in his frontal lobes and optimal norepinephrine levels in the brain. It says that when given Rorschach inkblots, he'd spend up to five minutes describing the scene. Much like you would a piece of art. But when they showed him a photo of a person, he'd give single-word answers: man, old, girl. Basically, he had little—if any—regard for human life. Let's see . . ." She read directly from the profile. "Confident to the point of arrogance, he fancies himself an art aficionado and philosopher. . . . Listen to this: 'Colonel Pushov displays many of the attributes of a borderline sociopath. Lacking any societal restraint, he will go to extreme lengths in order to achieve his goals. In combination with a dominant personality, this may lead to a significant lack of impulse control when it comes to the worth of human life.'"

Sydney flipped to another page.

"Pushov is old-school KGB. He is not above using civilians—women and children—to accomplish his tasks." Looking at the next page, Sydney scanned Victor's KGB mission history. "This guy is really scary," she said.

"Compared to what? The last dozen crazies we went up against?"

They sat quietly for a second. Vaughn looked over at Jack and Dixon, who both seemed engrossed in their reading. Leaning closer to Sydney, he murmured, "So, about what we were taking about, at your place? You come to any further conclusions about that?"

Smiling, Sydney continued to read the file. She had told herself that it wasn't the time and place, but Vaughn was asking questions that were definitely on her mind. "I don't know what I think. I've been trying to get my head around it for a long time, even before today. But every time I try . . . I don't know. . . ."

Vaughn tried unsuccessfully to hide his disappointment. It was obviously not the answer he was hoping for. "I can understand that." His hand covered hers. "If you ever want someone to talk to . . ."

"You too," Sydney replied, a faint smile on her lips. Vaughn smiled at her genuinely. Sydney just hoped that it was possible to get back to that place. So much had happened to them; it was going to be an extremely difficult task.

"No. That will not be sufficient. I want that information now," Sloane said into the phone. He looked up to see Nadia walking into his office, and he held his hand up to stop her before she could speak. "Yes, within the hour will be adequate." Sloane hung up the phone and turned his attention to his daughter. "I've been reaching out to my contacts in Eastern Europe, but no one seems to have any idea about what Pushov is up to. Have you and Marshall had any luck?"

"No. Nothing," Nadia said, all business. "We were able to compile a dossier on Pushov by accessing his military medical records, but there's nothing after the coup attempt. Marshall thinks he may be able to hack into the SVR/FSB intelligence database in order to find out what the Russians know. Weiss thinks he may have something from a previous contact of his who's now in custody. We're tightening the net."

"Sounds good." Sloane said.

Nadia just stood, silent, for a moment. She turned to leave, but stopped. "Why wasn't I sent to Prague?"

"Because you were needed here."

That is a typical Arvin Sloane statement, she thought, *true, yet not.* "I am better in the field. I'm a field agent," she said angrily.

"Nadia, everyone has a part to play here, and on this mission, yours is to support our team to the best of your ability. Are you going to be able to do that?"

Nadia tried to stare him down. But this was a game Sloane had played—for much higher stakes—many times. She finally backed down.

"Yes. I can do that," she answered, but didn't leave.

"Was there anything else?" Sloane asked.

"We'll let you know as soon as we get any more information."

"I ask for nothing more." He looked down at

the work spread out on his desk. Nadia turned to leave.

"Nadia?" he said.

She turned back, and Sloane rose from his chair to walk around his desk. "I was thinking that perhaps we could talk," he said.

"I've already told you no," Nadia retorted.

"I was hoping that maybe you had changed your mind," he said, catching Nadia off guard. She wasn't unaware of Sloane's desire to spend more time with her, but her mind was on the case at the moment, not on their family issues. "I was hoping that maybe we could go to dinner this weekend . . . ," he went on.

Her father looked feeble as he made his request. He looked as if he were a man near retirement, not a cold-blooded killer. But what frightened Nadia the most about it was his charm, how it still affected her.

She wanted to say so much. *I don't understand you. You met your daughter after more than twenty years, and what was the first thing you did? Gave her a hug? Told her that you loved her? No. You strapped her to a chair and injected her with toxins so that you could find something! And in the end you didn't even keep it. I don't understand you, how your head works. The only thing I do know is that I'm worth as much to you as something you ended up giving away.*

But Nadia didn't scream any of that. Instead they just stood there, neither one saying a thing. She shuffled the papers in her hand and said, "I need to follow up with Marshall on something."

Nadia turned and left her father's office. Arvin Sloane stood motionless in front of his desk and watched as she walked away.

CHAPTER 4

"How long has he been that way?" asked Victor, looking at the small monitor mounted above the worktable. A sharp Turkish cigarette dangled from his lips.

The fuzzy black-and-white image coming from the cheap Romanian copy of an early Sony television was clear enough to show Anton Sorokin sitting, asleep, in the chair. The night vision camera further bleached what was already a very pale image of the man in the cell.

"About three hours," replied the guard monitoring Sorokin.

Stubbing out his cigarette on the wall, Victor exhaled loudly. "Let's begin, shall we?"

Sorokin sat in the lone chair of his cell. After Victor had finished his tea, he'd left, taking the comfortable-looking chair with him. Five minutes later the lights had gone out. So Anton Sorokin sat in the dark. He knew the darkness was both deliberate and part of something bigger.

Damn it! Stop this train of thought. This is exactly what they want you to do: wear yourself down. It only makes their job easier.

Sorokin had sat there in the dark, trying to center himself, for what seemed like hours. Waiting for the inevitable.

When the door to his cell was unbolted, he was surprised to realize that he had fallen asleep. The lights, which seemed unusually bright, were flashed on, forcing his eyes to squint. Sorokin sat up as straight as he could. *Don't relinquish anything! They are animals, and they will use any signs of weakness to their advantage.* When the door opened, Sorokin wore the bravest face he could muster.

Victor entered the cell carrying his chair and,

more curiously, a small box. For a moment the two men just sat there, Victor in his soft chair and Sorokin in his uncomfortable one. And then a smile slowly began to appear on Victor's face. Although Sorokin refused to let his face show it, this slow smile unnerved him because, unlike previously, Victor's eyes smiled along with his lips. *What would excite such a twisted soul?* Sorokin wondered.

Every few seconds Victor's eyes flicked down to the box between them. He would watch Sorokin and then glance down to the box, obviously excited by whatever was inside. Sorokin found himself doing the same thing. And despite his best efforts, he could feel fear building inside of him. Just as Sorokin was sure he couldn't stand it anymore, Victor spoke.

"Are you wondering what I brought you, Anton?"

Sorokin could hear real joy in the man's voice. It was all he could do not to scream for help.

"Well, all I can say is that I think you'll be very interested in what is in here," Victor said. Then he pulled the lid off the box.

Before Sorokin dared look, his imagination spun out of control. *What is it? A nonvital part of my wife or daughter? The everyday tools he is going to use to torture me with?* Those terrible thoughts and a million other images flashed through his mind in the moment it took for Sorokin to gather the courage to look inside.

It was photographs!

Photographs of paintings.

Carefully, almost reverently, Victor lifted them out. Placing the box on the floor next to him, he set the photos down between them so that both men could look at them. Victor's face was alight with passion.

"These are my favorites." Victor pulled out four photographs and spread them out on the table. "I took all of these myself."

For a moment Sorokin questioned his captor's sanity. *Is this why he has taken me—to talk art?*

"Victor. You know I find these fascinating. But are you sure now is the time for this?" Sorokin asked gently.

Victor's smile didn't seem to dim in the least; in fact, it radiated a warmth that only startled Sorokin.

"This will only take a moment, Anton."

There was nothing Sorokin could do but look and listen.

"I was thinking about what you said to me when we were in your study . . . ," Victor began.

"You mean when you kidnapped me and my family?"

"I prefer the term *invited*." Victor pulled another photo out of the box and lined all five up in front of Sorokin. He continued, "So tell me, Anton, when you look at these pieces, what do you see?"

A confused look clouded Sorokin's face, but he had little choice. He carefully studied each photograph, then said, "I see five images of what are generally considered seminal works by five of the world's greatest artists. It could be said that these five pieces define classical art as we know it."

"Amazing." Sorokin could see the pleasure in Victor's face. "Almost verbatim from Roussierre's *Great Art of the Western World*. And it's true, these pieces have informed much of the art we see today. But I would take it a step further. I would propose that each of these works crossed the boundaries of the accepted work of its day, and therefore expanded it."

Victor slid one of the photos closer to Sorokin.

"Take this. Picasso's *Woman in Blue* was a radical departure from the mundane portraiture of the time."

"True," Sorokin said. "But he still worked with the paradigm of what is considered the postmodern aesthetic. The same could be said about all of these. Victor, I would have to say that although your theory has romantic flair, these works hardly support it."

Victor dug into the pile, obviously looking for a specific image. "I think I have something that may change your mind, Anton." He smiled, and he was still smiling when he placed a photograph in front of Sorokin. It wasn't of a painting; its subject was three-dimensional.

It was a photograph of Anna Sorokin.

She was dead.

At the sight of the image Sorokin went into shock. Nothing would move; his fingers could not grasp it. His hand could not tear it up. But worst of all, his eyes could not leave it.

Through the silent screams reverberating in his head, Anton Sorokin burned that image of his dead wife into his memory. It was then, through the haze of his astonishment, that he could hear Victor's voice.

"It's jarring, is it not? I took it myself, you know." Victor turned the photo to admire it. "It's cubist in nature. Harsh."

Sorokin could hear the man's words, but none

of them made any sense. The only thing that his shattered mind could process was a simple mantra of grief:

My wife.

Anna.

She's gone.

It beat over and over again through his brain as tears ran down his cheeks.

Victor carefully moved the photos away, but he left the one of Anna in front of his prisoner.

Sorokin's breathing ramped up. His soul was on fire. Victor's next words unbearably stoked the coals.

"Your daughter looks so much like her."

With that, Victor rose, lifted the box, and left the cell.

My wife.

Anna.

She's gone.

And my daughter?

Sorokin was left in the halls of the museum that Victor had created for him, repeating over and over again his personal tragedy. The loss of light in the room, the loss of light in his life.

* * *

Victor stood in front of the cheap Romanian monitor watching Anton Sorokin hit rock bottom. Reaching into his pocket, he pulled out another sharp Turkish cigarette and lit it. He took a deep, satisfying drag and exhaled, never taking his eyes off Sorkin. "He's almost ready for his task."

CHAPTER 5

The bag was made of heavy black plastic, designed to keep prying eyes out and the morbid aromas of death in. It was two meters long and half as wide. Bright yellow and red biohazard symbols strategically placed were purposely a sharp contrast to the dark bag. Sydney hoped this would discourage any unwanted inspections.

She leaned back in the passenger seat of the Bollanti ambulance she and Dixon were to drive to their mission. She had learned in her time as a spy that no matter what country, village, or metropolitan city she was in, real-life items had wear and tear. Matchbook edges should be crinkled on the corners, local currency should never be shiny. She smiled inwardly, recalling a time when she and Marshall stood shivering in an all-night Laundromat in Kyoto, ignoring the curious stares of the other patrons as their dryer thumped with their shoes, plastic toys, and coats, all mixed with half a billion counterfeit yen. *Wear and tear made it real,* she thought.

It was this rationale that made her appreciate the watermarks, heat damage, and general look of use on the body bag before her. After one more glance, she determined it worthy of her standards.

As her eyes flicked from the gurney to the front of the vehicle, she found a comforting sight. Dixon watched over her as she processed her alias and its accuracy. Sydney knew the look he was imparting to her quite well. It implied luck, strength, trust, and, most important, *Come back in one piece.*

She smiled as she tucked her hair back behind her ear, then affixed her name tag to the white, mid-thigh-length overcoat she wore. The seam was frayed near her left shoulder. It fit loosely over a pair of black pants and a tight black shirt.

She noted as she attached her ID that Marshall

had done his usual exceptional job forging her papers: a laminated photo of Sydney with a Russian name and various approval signatures all imprinted with the watermarked symbol of the Moscow Board of Medical Examiners. Sydney had worried that one of the last names looked misspelled, but Marshall assured her that in a six-month period, four hundred identifications had been issued with a misspelled police administrator's name. *He is a gem,* Sydney thought.

It definitely looked legitimate. She had studied the mortuary blueprints enough to front that she had dropped off deceased cargo before.

Dixon put a billed cap on his head, one that perfectly matched the medical examiner uniform he was wearing.

"You look ten years younger in that cap," Sydney said in Russian, realizing she was hitting her *R*s too hard for a native speaker—a detail she tweaked even as the words rolled off her tongue.

"I'll wear it around the office." Dixon smiled as if to say, *I wish I meant that,* then threw the relic of a van he was piloting in motion.

Acquiring the medical examiner's van had been surprisingly easy and a little unnerving. Jack Bristow had taken them to an aging ex-KGB contact now working as a lowly security guard. Sydney guessed that there wasn't much work for secret police thugs in the new Russia. Jack handed the man a roll of five thousand weathered euros, and the man handed him the keys to the van. The unnerving part of the transaction was that the man said for an extra twenty-five hundred he could supply bodies for added authenticity. Jack had declined.

Dixon popped the clutch, changed gears, and with one last look at himself in the rearview mirror, brought the medical examiner's van through the wrought-iron archway with a sign that read FOREVER IN PEACE in Cyrillic. Dixon marveled at the Gothic beauty of the place. The mortuary itself sat five miles from the bustling streets of Prague's urban business district. The location was perfect because it was just far enough away to escape immediate suspicion, yet close enough to the most important government buildings to make surveillance possible.

As they weaved closer to the main building of the sprawling cemetery, the city was visible in the distance. The spires of the old churches poked out of the hazy noontime air. It was typical Czech weather, with a definite chill.

Sydney noticed spires coming out of the ground; gray structures reminiscent of stalagmites poked through the green grass. Square headstones with iron face plates were too numerous to count. Most eye-catching of all were the mausoleums with copper roofs that were now a permanent swirl of oxidized green, which dotted the landscape like large, cement tree trunks. There were few real trees, so most of the grounds were visible in a panoramic sweep. It was calming for mourners, and tactically practical for Victor Pushov's operation to keep lookout.

Near the main building a gathering of a few dozen people in shades of black and gray surrounded a coffin, mourning a loved one.

Dixon drove the van up to the rear of the main building. As he did, Sydney picked up the large Styrofoam cup sitting in the console to her right. Removing the lid, she released the pungent aroma of Halászlé, a hearty fish soup. Taking a deep gulp, she washed it around her mouth before swallowing. She grimaced horribly and wondered how something so unpalatable was such a common dish. She leaned toward Dixon and asked, "How's this?"

Pulling back, his face a mask of revulsion,

Dixon said, "Like something died in your mouth."

"That's the idea."

Opening her lip balm, Sydney removed a small transceiver about the size of an aspirin. When the two halves of the device were twisted, the wireless splice turned on. She placed it in her pocket and noticed out the tinted windows that the mortuary was in sight.

Dixon cautiously backed the vehicle up to the building's adjoining ramp. A sign posted on the wall indicated that this was the entrance for bodies to be delivered. Almost instantly a man appeared at the driver's side window with a clipboard in hand. The guard wore black pants and a jacket that protected a blue collared shirt underneath. The most notice-able attributes of this business uniform were the white ID card attached to his left lapel, and the old load ink well pen that the man pushed squarely at Dixon's face. Dixon scrawled a signature, quickly giving the impression that he was even less inter-ested than the man handing the clipboard to him.

In a flash, Sydney was out of the van and unloading the gurney. A second man approached immediately under the guise of offering help. In reality, Sydney knew, he wanted to get a look at the new girl. His advances were met with her stern Russian tongue. "You want to help me? Then get the door open up there."

The man froze for half a second. Although Sydney was beautiful, with short, raven-colored hair, her blue eyes and natural attractiveness were neutralized by possibly the worst breath he had ever smelled. Her demeanor was all business, her look was successfully commonplace, and her pronunciation of *R*s could have placed her voice seamlessly in any open-air market in Moscow.

"Today, please." Sydney continued up the ramp as the man snapped out of his I-need-to-get-a-better-look-at-her curves reverie. He rushed ahead and gave a signal to someone she could see inside. She watched as a man behind a podium hit a button in the wall that electronically flung open the doors before her. Sydney noted to herself that the doors needed to be released from a private station. An agent should always know where to exit. Leaving could always become a problem later.

The man watched her go, and the doors closed with Sydney safely inside. Dixon suppressed a smile as the morgue attendant approached him. After sharing a knowing look that said, yes, she was the most attractive medical examiner they had seen in months, Dixon pulled out an aluminum clipboard to begin his "paperwork."

"Hey you can't stay here," said the morgue attendant who moments ago had directed Sydney into the building. "Park on the street. I'll tell her where you went."

Dixon looked the man in the face and knew that he wasn't going to talk him into letting him stay. Grumbling in Czech, he saluted farewell and pulled the vehicle a short distance away from the mortuary to set himself in the best position he could under the circumstances. He pulled a laptop computer from underneath the seat and turned it on. As it booted up he repositioned the van so that he could watch the entrance, monitor the people who came and went, and, if need be, pull the weapon from the back and provide cover for Sydney's escape.

Sydney's footsteps echoed as her shoes connected with the marble floor of the mortuary. The steady rhythm alerted anyone in earshot that someone was approaching. The wheels of the gurney rolled along almost smoothly. Hours earlier she had kicked the front right wheel, damaging it just enough to show that although it was broken, Sydney had complete knowledge of her gurney's shortcomings. She made minor corrections as she pushed it quickly. Her demeanor said that she had a busy day and that this inconvenience was just one of many.

She was stopped by a man at a small podium desk. He sat in a raised chair behind the small workstation. He was dressed like the guard outside, but with one difference: a Glock 17 was positioned in a holster under his coat. Sydney knew the bulge such a weapon would make, but then again, by the look of the guard before her, that was probably the point he was trying to get across.

His name tag simply read NIKOLAV. No last name.

He was a foot taller and wider than Sydney. His small eyes were set deep in his large head, which gave the impression that he was constantly staring. His narrow lips peeked through a beard. All Sydney could think of was how he should be standing next to a velvet rope. He would make the perfect bouncer.

"Stop." Nikolav said mechanically. Sydney could now see that he had a small bank of monitors before him. There were four small screens, each with its own black-and-white display. Sydney noticed that every ten seconds the scene would switch to views of other positions in the mortuary subbasements. Sydney hid her worry at the image of a man patrolling with a machine gun resting on a tattered shoulder strap.

Sydney pulled her gum out of her mouth with her left hand. Once she dropped her hand to her side, she wedged the little transceiver inside it. She gave Nikolav a fake smile and then tossed her gum in an adjacent trash can.

"I've got a juicy one here," Sydney said. Before Nikolav could reply, Sydney tossed her name badge onto his sign-in sheet, adding, "Paperwork says drop him off downstairs. Sublevel two."

"You can't go down there. You'll have to wait while I go."

With that information, Sydney unzipped the body bag about three inches, and a *scent* was emitted. Nikolav recoiled from the rancid attack on his nostrils.

Sydney reminded herself to compliment Marshall on a job well done when she got back. He had expressed great fervor in creating the sensory gadget whose inspiration was one part his son's diapers, one part wet dog, and two parts rotting meat. Marshall had spring-loaded the scent's release into the zipper of the body bag. It was a one-time use gag. "But a convincing argument only needs to be heard once," he had promised. And it turned out, he was right.

Sydney flopped two large black gloves onto the top of the bag. In response to Nikolav's insistence that he take the body down himself, she said, "Fine by me. But I need all four pieces stored properly and my gloves back, sanitized, thank you."

With that, Nikolav waved her through. Sydney paused for half a beat to impress upon him a sneer of disapproval. Once she was past him he turned to watch her, but he was distracted by the clacking of the broken gurney wheel.

Sydney now focused on the elevator up ahead. With her thumb she stealthily loosened her middle finger press-on nail, painted black to match her hair. She worked it back and forth as she waited for the elevator doors to open up before her.

Nikolav had frozen the camera monitor on her getting into the elevator. What he didn't know was that the transceiver in her discarded gum worked as a small wireless Internet hub. Its range was a mere seven feet, but it was wide enough to encompass the electronics that ran Nikolav's monitors. Thanks to the device, Dixon could now monitor from the laptop in the van.

Sydney's press-on nail tilted forward to reveal the smallest of microchips. *So far, so good,* she thought as the elevator arrived and she entered it with the gurney.

Once Sydney was inside the elevator, Dixon overrode the camera angles on the monitoring station. He began running a program that looped images, recycling ten-second clips from various video intakes to mask Sydney's true position.

Just as the elevator started to descend Sydney received clearance from Dixon. She quickly unzipped the body bag. It contained tactical gear, two machine guns, and her greatest asset in the field . . . Agent Michael Vaughn.

CHAPTER 6

Despite being encased in a body bag, Vaughn was, in fact, very much alive. It hadn't been easy for him to lie still, listening to Sydney execute their entrance on her own. Not one to sit idly, he was in motion the moment she opened the bag. Motivating him wasn't just a sense of duty and survival, but Sydney herself. The woman he desperately loved was his responsibility. He felt remorse for his time spent with Lauren, not simply for the hurt that he had put Sydney through, but also, as he learned the truth, the danger he had put her in. But in the aftermath he was a new and, in his mind, *better* agent. One that he hoped could do a much more thorough job of protecting what he cherished most in the world—Sydney Bristow.

Dressed in dark blue worker pants and a fitted sweater, Vaughn adjusted his headset and clicked off his weapon's safety. "The chip."

"I'm on it," Sydney replied. She took out a Swiss Army knife, but instead of the standard blade, it housed a skeleton key. In one smooth motion she unlocked the elevator's electrical box. Not missing a beat, she then slid the minuscule computer chip, hidden under her middle fingernail, directly into the electronic switchboard.

"I'm overriding the elevator display now," said Dixon's reassuring voice over their headsets.

Nikolav held an apple in his hand. He'd been eyeing the elevator, or more accurately, the iron display arrow positioned above its doors. The display registered five floors; the ground floor where Nikolav stood guard, and four sublevels. Nikolav watched the metal arrow move to the second subbasement level—exactly where the pretty yet bossy woman told him she was headed. Satisfied, he resumed eating the apple.

* * *

The elevator doors opened onto the lowest underground basement. Vaughn was out the door quicker than Sydney would have liked. Instantaneously she weighed his rogue actions of late against his recent promise in her apartment. *I want to believe you, Michael,* she told herself. *I'm nothing if I abandon my hope in others.* But now in the field, where time was always a concern, she could not justify reflecting any further. Vaughn motioned to her that it was clear to proceed.

In contrast to the marble upstairs, the subbasement was all neglected concrete floor and bare cinder block walls. Lighting was sporadic at best. As her eyes took in the layout, Sydney recalled the mortuary's blueprints she had memorized on the plane trip over.

The elevator doors closed behind her. Dixon's voice immediately confirmed, "Elevator is locked down. It won't move until I make it move."

With the agreed-upon protocols in place, Vaughn nodded to Sydney. They moved seamlessly. From afar one would see it as a ballet of precision. This was the pair at their best. Sydney knew it, as did Vaughn. And they both wished that life outside of APO operated as smoothly.

Suddenly Vaughn caught sight of a guard just crossing ahead.

"I'm going north," Vaughn said sharp and low. "Careful, Sydney."

She gave a nod as a response, her face a mask of determination.

"We rendezvous here in ten minutes."

And with those words, Vaughn moved stealthily out of sight. Alone, Sydney noticed for the first time just how quiet it was down there.

Vaughn found himself at a corner near a bank of deserted offices. Down at the end of the hall he saw a guard positioned at a small wooden desk. Cluttered atop the desk were a telephone; a laptop; a cheap, plastic desk lamp; and an old black-and-white, rabbit-eared television. The guard used the nose of his machine gun to make a slight angular tweak to the antenna. From the audio Vaughn could tell he was watching a soccer match.

Vaughn turned back around the corner and quietly spoke into comms. "Phoenix, have you found anything?"

Silence. Something was not right.

Then Sydney answered and he relaxed, until he

absorbed her actual words. Her voice was small, controlled. "I've found Sorokin's wife. . . . She's dead."

Sydney was in an embalming room. Even with only the glow of a small flashlight, the room's rundown state was unmistakable. The walls and floor were dirty. Several freezer doors were unhinged. The room, in short, was rank. A quick assessment of the space showed that it was reminiscent of places better left in nightmares. Sydney wanted nothing more than to leave.

Instead, she stood in the center of the room, where four stainless steel tables were stationed, each topped with a corpse.

Examining the bodies more closely, Sydney identified the female corpse closest to her as the fallen undercover CIA agent. Sydney gazed at the young woman's pale face, recalling from the file she had read on the plane that this woman was someone's sister, daughter, and girlfriend. Death was hard enough to witness without knowing its victim's personal information.

The next two bodies were men. One had several bullet wounds to the chest, and the other appeared to have been stabbed to death.

And on the final table lay the body of Anna Sorokin. Even in death, a proud look remained on her face. Sydney projected that it was a defiant glare at the evil that had done this to her. Sydney looked at her stoically, empathetically, and with a great sadness. Innocent death was the worst sort of collateral damage in her profession. Just then her thoughts were curtailed by Vaughn's voice.

"Any sign of the other two?"

"Not yet," she answered.

"I don't like it down here. Let's find them and clear out." There was a pause, and then Vaughn's whispered voice returned, laced with urgency. "A second guard is on the move."

This was information Sydney was already aware of. She'd crouched down under a bank of windows that looked out into the hallway, and she could see the guard's shadow walking outside. To her alarm, the shadow paused directly over where she was crouched. Sydney prayed that it was just a routine check and the guard would continue on his rounds.

If they were discovered now, they'd fail to retrieve Anton and Faina Sorokin. And if the guard alerted the compound, their escape would be most difficult. Even if they could get to the minister and his daughter, the very nature of being underground would make it nearly impossible to extract themselves without a fierce fight. The only exit was a good twenty meters above them.

Please, just walk on. . . .

A beat later, the guard's shadow trailed off.

Sydney cautiously peered through the grimy window glass. Satisfied she was alone again, she returned to her examination of Anna Sorokin's body. There were bruises and contusions on Anna's right cheek, left arm, and upper thigh. Sydney found dead skin underneath the woman's fingernails. *She didn't go without a fight.* A bullet hole was in her chest, on her right side; she probably bled to death.

A silver cameo necklace hung from Mrs. Sorokin's neck. It was simple yet elegant. Although the urgency of her mission was tugging her away, there was one more thing Sydney had to know.

With a deep breath, she opened the locket. Inside was a photo of a girl, around twelve years old, with a fire for life burning in her smile. *Faina.*

On the other side of the pendant she expected to find a picture of Anton, but instead of another photo, there was a small crayon drawing, in shades of green, brown, and purple.

A shadow and the sound of footsteps approached the room.

Another guard, damn it!

Frantically she looked for a place to hide. *There's nowhere to go!*

Ten seconds later a guard entered the embalming room. He stopped a foot inside, surveying the collection of bodies with his flashlight. Pointing it around the room, the flashlight lit the most obvious places anyone might choose to hide: under the tables and in a two-foot slot between two chemical storage closets. All the while dust particles danced within the illuminated circle. The guard worked the light deliberately, slowly, making sure he was satisfied before he would move on.

Sydney was above him. Her arms and legs wedged her body perfectly in the corner above the door frame. Her shoulder-length hair hung down on either side of her face.

She didn't dare breathe. She told herself, *Keep still, keep quiet, keep balance. . . .*

Finally the guard beneath her shook his head and left the room. She could hear his footsteps retreating. Waiting several moments longer than even she knew was necessary, Sydney exhaled. Her toned physique just now began to feel the strain of holding her weight in complete and utter silence.

That was close.

Something unusual caught Vaughn's eye through an open office door. While the rest of the floor displayed clear signs of neglect and abandonment, this particular office's worktable had been recently used. Stamped on its dusty surface was the distinct outline of a laptop. Remnants of wire and soldering coil had left fresh burn marks beside it. And most curious was a piece of fabric left behind.

Vaughn quietly entered the room and picked up the rough scrap of fabric. He'd worn enough Kevlar to recognize its feel. It smelled new. He pocketed it and focused his attention on the table's burn marks. His investigation was cut short by the sound of Sydney's voice in his ear.

"Shotgun?" she said.

He walked back into the hall. "Go ahead," he replied.

"I found the girl."

Vaughn looked up. A guard was standing right before him, gun drawn. Vaughn, too, had been found.

Sydney was in a darkened corner of the basement. Fresh footprints had led her to the area. Along the left-hand wall were a series of heavy metal doors. The first one revealed the facility's crematory. The second had a small window in its door, and through the six-inch glass Sydney first glimpsed a piece of hope.

She recognized Faina Sorokin—alive and well—instantly. Despite being confined to a cell, she exuded very much the spark contained in the photo Sydney had taken off her mother before she left the embalming room. Faina was sitting on the floor, knees to her chest, deeply focused in thought. She was petite and thin, but she could hardly be described as frail. With dark brown hair and piercing green eyes, the seventeen-year-old Faina reminded Sydney of someone she knew.

A nanosecond later it hit her. She was looking at herself. Young, beautiful, full of hope and sorrow, entwined in a ball of imprisonment.

This troubled her. Sydney wasn't quite sure whether that was because she hated to see anyone else go through what she had suffered, or because seeing Faina reopened her own childhood wounds. Sydney worked so hard to leave the past in the past. It was hard enough seeing Arvin Sloane every day and living with the reminders of Danny and Francie all over Los Angeles. She pushed these thoughts away. Right now she needed to get Faina out and still find her father.

"My name is Sydney," she announced. "I'm here to get you out."

As proof of her intent, Sydney waved her skeleton key, only to see Faina studying her. Others would barter things both great and small just to have someone utter those words and mean them. But Faina cooly looked up at Sydney and defiantly said, "I'm not leaving without my parents."

The guard facing Vaughn looked slightly hesitant, as if he was trying to decide if he should first contact his superiors or subdue the intruder. Vaughn had learned that hesitation was a person's greatest weakness, and he used the split-second opportunity to attack. In a few swift motions Vaughn knocked the enemy's gun aside and had the guard in a crippling chokehold. Despite some flailing,

Vaughn soon had deadweight in his arms.

Quickly Vaughn used the unconscious guard's belt to bind his hands, and then used a torn piece of the man's shirt as a makeshift gag. *Not bad,* he thought as he surveyed his handiwork.

Suddenly the guard's walkie-talkie came to life, emitting emotional chatter in Russian. *Sydney!* But then he realized that the excitement only concerned the televised soccer match, not the discovery or capture of the intruders.

Relieved, Vaughn checked comms. "Phoenix, what's your twenty?"

"The crematory," Sydney replied.

"I'm on my way."

Sydney and Faina stood in front of the open door of a second cell. It was empty and its lone seat was cold. No other holding cells had been found.

"Where are my parents?" Faina asked, not for the first time.

"We're looking for them," promised Sydney, trying to reassure the frustrated teenager.

"I haven't seen my mother since yesterday, and three hours ago I heard guards speaking about moving my father."

"We'll keep searching, but first we need to rejoin my partner and get you to safety."

"But I'm not leaving without—"

Sydney held her hand up and the girl instantly stopped talking. Two sets of footsteps were approaching. . . .

Where are you, Vaughn?

Vaughn retraced his steps and found a new guard watching the television set. The distracted guard tilted his head and asked, "Peter, is that you? You won't believe the score. . . ."

Even with the element of surprise, Vaughn's chokehold was less effective this time. This guard knew a thing or two about hesitation.

The guard immediately jabbed Vaughn in the ribs. Vaughn buckled, but maintained his hold on the man. Another elbow shot loosened Vaughn's grip just enough for the guard to pull his gun from the holster.

If he gets a round off, this whole thing is blown!

Vaughn grabbed the man's gun hand and snapped the wrist like it was peanut brittle. Sharp pain sent the guard into shock. Vaughn used the moment to land a crushing blow to the guard's temple, effectively taking out his adversary.

As quickly and quietly as possible, Vaughn propped the guard into the chair as if the poor guy had simply dozed off in front of the soccer match. This was taking too much time. He needed to regroup with Sydney and get them out before any more trouble followed.

By crouching beside the table, Sydney and Faina evaded discovery by a pair of passing sentries. *For the moment,* Sydney thought. But then she spotted something else. She tried to hide the blood, but Faina immediately noticed the crimson marks dotting the crematory's rickety table. There were also trace amounts of blood on the cracked tile floor and flecks on the wall. Sydney watched as each discovery registered with greater and greater horror on the girl's face.

Reading her thoughts, Sydney lied to her. "We don't know for sure—"

Faina pushed past her, running her index finger along the largest dot of blood. It wasn't wet, but it still had tackiness to it. Turning to Sydney, there was nothing left for Faina to say.

Anton Sorokin was no longer there. *Why? Why leave the daughter? And where did they go?* Too many questions. Worse than her capture was Faina's separation from her family. She was devastated. Bringing down Victor Pushov was part of her mission, but more then anything right now, Sydney wanted the chance to wash the past thirty-six hours away from Faina's mind.

Then rage replaced Faina's fear. "Where the *hell* are my parents?"

Sydney knew then that it was time to go. "We have to leave—"

Looking behind Sydney, Faina screamed.

CHAPTER 7

It was Faina's wide-eyed stare more than anything else that confirmed for Sydney that they were under attack.

Sydney's muscles reacted on pure instinct. She dropped into a crouch—a simple trick that made her a smaller target. Twisting her upper torso toward her attacker allowed her to focus her strength into a fully extended roundhouse kick. The heel of her heavy work boot caught her attacker squarely on the side of his head, driving him back.

It was then that she saw the second man.

Sydney and he exchanged a series of blows and defensive blocks. Sydney fought with a ferocity born from an adrenaline rush. Her fighting style was aggressive, at times even seemingly reckless. On the other hand, the guard's fighting skills were clearly reactive.

Sydney used this to her advantage.

Pushing him back with a barrage of punches and kicks, she found the opening she was looking for. With an overshot punch, her out-of-breath opponent momentarily lost his balance. That one misstep was all Sydney needed.

She moved in with amazing speed, clutching his throat tightly with her right hand.

But just when she felt sure of her grip and of her control of the situation, a blinding pain came from her side.

The first guard had rejoined the fight and landed a sharp strike to her right kidney. The impact made her let go of the other man and stagger back.

But there was no time for pain. Within seconds she returned two right crosses to the first guard's face and a left jab to his stomach, and then with a two-handed shove, pushed him backward into a stainless steel worktable on wheels. The man clumsily toppled to the ground. Sydney rushed over to continue her attack, only to find that the guard was unconscious. Momentarily relieved, she felt the second attacker closing in behind her.

Spinning around, Sydney grabbed the man's right arm and slammed it over the edge of an old filing cabinet, audibly snapping his wrist. Wrenching free, he cursed at her in Russian. The two circled each other like jungle cats, the man wincing from his broken wrist and Sydney trying to ignore the throbbing in her side.

We don't have time for this. More could arrive at any moment.

The guard moved in with a fake jab, but Sydney deftly grabbed his arm, using his body's momentum against him. With him now off-balance, Sydney drove her elbow into his nose, breaking it with a *crunch* and driving him backward. Next she spun her body to take him out with a final roundhouse kick, but to her surprise, he still had more fight left!

Avoiding her kick, the man lunged at Sydney, wrapping his arms around her body as if his only goal now was to squeeze the life out of her. One of her arms was pinned. She knew she had a narrowing window to counter his attack before she lost consciousness.

Sydney's eyes sought Faina, who watched, terrified, from across the room. *This has gone on long enough. I need to get her out of here now!*

Sydney drove her free elbow up into her attacker's temple, but the determined man would not let go. Switching methods, she kicked backward, driving her boot heel sharply into the man's knee. There was an audible *crack,* but the man remarkably still did not let go. Instead, with rage-filled eyes, he retaliated by forcefully shoving her head into the bricks of the crematory furnace.

Sydney's world went black for half a second.

Desperately struggling to breathe, Sydney once again drove her elbow into his face. A second later she found herself sprawled out on the furnace's conveyer belt.

The man came up behind her and reached down to clutch her throat with both hands.

Instinct summoned a well-placed kick to the man's throat. Choking from the unexpected blow, he staggered back, bumping into the cremation control panel.

The conveyer belt—pulling a stunned Sydney—

started moving along the track in the direction of the oven. Still trying to shake the cobwebs from her head, Sydney could feel the sudden intense heat emanating from the awakened furnace. She tried to get back on her feet.

But at that moment her opponent slammed her flat, using his weight against her. He was above her, walking alongside the moving belt. The searing heat of the flames and the smell of gas drew very close as Sydney continued to roll backward toward the open oven.

Only a second to act!

Instead of trying to push her attacker away, Sydney grabbed on to him, pulling him toward her and off his feet. The surprise tactic allowed her to use the force of his body to help her tuck and roll off the other side of the conveyer belt's platform.

Sydney anticipated that he would immediately join her and continue the fight, but she heard him cry out instead. His right sleeve had caught on the conveyer belt's chain. He struggled with his uniform's thick fabric, but it would neither tear nor come loose. Overcome, he turned to Sydney in horror.

It was over before Sydney could truly comprehend the awful reality of it. One moment the guard was struggling on the table, and in the blink of an eye he was engulfed within a blanket of flames. The man's screams were unbearable.

Running to the control panel, Sydney frantically looked for the kill switch. And then she saw it—a key that needed to be turned clockwise ninety degrees. But to Sydney's horror, it was broken off, undoubtedly a casualty of their preceding fight.

But even worse than the man's screams was seeing Faina's catatonic reaction. Her tear-streaked face glowed orange from the flames' reflection.

All Sydney could do was stagger over and slam the furnace door shut, hoping to wipe the image of death from Faina's mind.

But the stench of charred flesh still filled the room. Her heart pounding, Sydney forced herself to focus. The man was gone.

Save the girl.

Vaughn ran as fast as he could. The last thing he heard from Sydney was labored breathing before the connection went dead. He queried sharply, but his requests were only met with silence.

At the crematory—Sydney's last known whereabouts—he was relieved to find her alive and with Sorokin's daughter. But both of them appeared to be in shock—the daughter, Faina, in particular. The room felt tense, and Vaughn couldn't place the horrible smell in the air.

Holstering his weapon, Vaughn spoke as gently as possible. "Sydney?"

Sydney's eyes turned to him. Vaughn could tell by the look that now was not the time to ask what had happened. Currently they had a more pressing matter: getting out of this basement alive. First Vaughn checked the body of a guard crumpled next to the wall. He was out cold.

"We'd better get out of here," Vaughn said.

Sydney's eyes came back into complete focus as she surveyed the destroyed room. "Neither had a chance to sound the alarm, but they'll be missed soon," she said matter-of-factly.

Neither? he wanted to ask, noting only one unconscious guard. There would be time to ask what had happened once they got out. *If* they got out. That's when the girl started up.

"You killed him!" Faina screamed, walking toward Sydney. A look of revulsion on her face. "You threw him in that furnace and burned him alive!"

Vaughn looked from the blasting furnace to Sydney, the reality sinking in. Sydney looked away uncomfortably.

"We need to leave. Now," Sydney said gravely.

"We can't leave!" cried Faina. She was clearly on the edge of hysteria.

Vaughn looked at Faina. *She's losing it, and we don't have time for this.*

"Sorokin?" asked Sydney.

Vaughn shook his head. "They must've already moved him."

Faina now got into Vaughn's face. "We can look on another—"

Vaughn shook his head. "No time. The security teams will find out their friends are missing any minute."

"What about my fath—"

Sydney picked up her weapon. Checking her clip, she looked at Vaughn. "You're right. We have to leave now."

"Don't you two listen?!" Faina cried, her complexion darkening with anger. "I'm not leaving without my parents!"

Vaughn watched as Sydney tried unsuccessfully to rationalize with the girl. Time was already against them, and Faina's screaming wasn't helping them stay undetected.

While Sydney still tried to reason with the young girl, Vaughn grabbed a large piece of packing gauze off the stainless steel countertop below some medicine cabinets. Searching through adjacent bottles, he found what he was looking for: fulminate or hydrochloric acid. Sydney held the girl's hand in an effort to calm her, but she wasn't having it. Meanwhile Vaughn found the other half of his idea— pure ether. Carefully he poured small amounts of each onto a tattered piece of the gauze, holding his breath so he would not inhale the vapors.

Vaughn then crept up to Faina, and before she could say another word, he placed the piece of gauze over her nose and mouth. Faina's eyes burst wide in fright, but soon her muffled screams stopped and she slumped into his arms.

Sydney watched wide-eyed, her legs frozen to the ground. "What did you do to her?!"

"We don't have time to baby her," Vaughn replied, shifting Faina in his arms.

"So how are we going to get her out of here?"

Vaughn threw the girl over his shoulder. "I've got an idea."

Suddenly static-filled Russian voices came from the walkie-talkie attached to the unconscious guard's belt loop.

Vaughn and Sydney exchanged a look.

A second of silence followed, and then by the urgent tone of the voices, one didn't even need to know Russian to understand the imminent danger.

More guards would be on the scene in minutes.

Vaughn returned Sydney's stare. *It's now or never.*

As the elevator rose toward the receiving area, Dixon reconnected with Sydney.

"We need some help here," she said via their comms. "Potential exit may be compromised."

Dixon was in the back of the van already working on a solution; he had been following the mission on his monitors. "Roger, Phoenix. I'm already moving on it."

Quickly tapping the laptop's keys, Dixon released the elevator controls. He then swiftly rotated through the dozen or so monitors in the basement areas and saw the Russians beginning to react to their missing men. By the time he got back to the elevator cam, Vaughn was hidden again in the black body bag. Satisfied that Sydney's alias was restored, he released the camera program at Nikolav's podium.

Perfectly executed, all Nikolav would see was an attractive Russian woman with short, jet-black hair, not pleased in any way as to how her day was progressing. In addition, Dixon manipulated the camera shots to skip over any implicating views. Removal of incriminating angles would hopefully create a few extra seconds for them to escape. Nikolav would be none the wiser.

The last thing Dixon did before he left the van was release "the mole." The mole was a little program that Marshall had written for just such an emergency. It was like an electronic time bomb that, once released into a computer system, would silently disable any alarm system and then in seven minutes, overwhelm the entire IT system, including the telephones and wireless communication hubs.

Now that the program was running, Dixon tossed his baseball cap onto the seat next to him. In one motion, his overcoat and ID badge were removed. Then, reaching under his seat, he pulled out a small bouquet of flowers. The arrangement was deliberately purchased from a stand only a mile away to match those already placed on gravestones by local relatives and friends.

Dixon scanned the area as he exited the van, mentally tagging the most probable threats and potential escape routes. It was a habit that kept him alive.

As he walked toward the entrance of the mortuary, dressed in an inconspicuous gray coat, he was constantly on the lookout for any clue of trouble; anything at all that might be out of the ordinary. *The groundskeeper trimming a hedge has no other maintenance tools. The couple standing over a grave marker seem more interested in the crowd than their deceased relative. Is the building being locked down?*

Dixon pushed in behind a large group of people listening to a eulogy. Up front was the gray casket that he and Sydney had seen during their drive up. An older man in a black suit was giving a speech. Some of the mourners sobbed, others consoled those who were upset, but the majority stood in silence. Dixon noted that the eulogy was not in Czech, but Lithuanian.

To the casual observer, Dixon was listening to the eulogy. Only someone as well trained as Dixon would be able to tell that he was in fact counting the employees milling around the mortuary's receiving entrance. Searching casually, he shifted over to the back of the crowd. By the time the minister asked the group to bow their heads and pray, Dixon had seen what he needed to. With determination to aid his friends, he moved in.

As the elevator doors opened on the ground floor, Sydney instantly resumed the persona she had presented to Nikolav. The ease of the transformation always slightly unsettled her—the ability to appear wholeheartedly honest while telling bold-faced lies.

A true pro knew that it was usually the eyes that gave someone away. Sydney had had witnessed her father on several occasions give a lie detector test sans that machine, opting only to look deeply into the subject's eyes for the truth.

Right now Sydney's eyes said many things. Nikolav would later tell his friends that the woman had a spark, but it was fueled with the disgust of dealing with a particular case on a bad day. Her eyes said that this job was only until something better came along.

The gurney's broken wheel announced her presence before Nikolav even looked up. One of his meaty hands jutted out into the walkway like a stop sign as Sydney neared his workstation. Nikolav greeted Sydney with a sly smile. His eyes noted her return cargo.

"I see you still have the body," he said smugly.

Playing into Nikolav's condescending attitude, Sydney replied in Russian, "Are you paid to be obvious, or is that an emerging talent?"

The man smirked. "Your client doesn't care for the accommodations?"

Sydney offered him a look of impatient annoyance. "Your man downstairs tells me he will not take this body. So it looks like I wasted the trip."

Nikolav stepped in front of the gurney, forcing Sydney to stop.

The exit was no more then ten feet behind him.

"I need to confirm your friend's identity," said Nikolav.

Sydney knew this was not usual protocol. The bored guard was creating an excuse to keep talking to a pretty stranger.

"Are you nuts?" Sydney said indignantly. "I'm already late without another delay."

Nikolav chuckled as Sydney saw another guard approach the elevator behind her. The elevator doors opened and he stepped inside. It would be at most two minutes before everything fell apart.

As Sydney formulated a plan to get out as safely as possible, she noted two more guards approaching her rapidly. Taped beneath the edge of the gurney was her handgun. Trying not to draw attention, she moved her hand closer to the weapon, ready to escape by sheer force if necessary.

But instead of reassuring her, Sydney saw the last thing she wanted to see.

A few inches of dark hair was visible below the wool blanket that now draped over the gurney, beneath the body bag. Like her hand gun, she and Vaughn had strapped Faina to the underside of the gurney to conceal her from Nikolav's scrutinizing eyes.

"This has been the worst day . . . ," Sydney intentionally muttered under her breath, just audible enough for Nikolav to hear. She stepped a few inches closer to Nikolav's station, blocking his view of the gurney.

Nikolav asked her about signing paperwork. It was becoming increasingly difficult to maintain her casual demeanor. *If anyone spotted the hair . . .*

She avoided eye contact with the two approaching men. Then, as Nikolav handed Sydney a clipboard to sign, he stopped.

A distraught mourner entered, his eyes red and swollen.

It was Dixon!

Unexpectedly Dixon clutched one of the guard's arms. In broken Russian, he tried to convey his loss, his pain, and his need to speak to someone about his dead son. Sydney couldn't help but recall that she had seen this display before; it was a reprise of Dixon's grief following his wife's death.

Suddenly Nikolav had the clipboard forced back into his hand. Sydney passed Dixon, and the guards shook him off on their way toward the elevator. The guards' walkie-talkies began to squawk that there was a problem.

Outside the electronic double doors, the getaway van was now in Sydney's line of sight. She willed herself toward it.

Eight feet to go . . .

Five feet . . .

Then suddenly Nikolav called out, "Excuse me. . . . Excuse me. Stop!"

Sydney ignored him and closed the remaining

gap to the exit doors. She knew Nikolav had to operate the master release button at his podium. *Please, Vaughn, stay still. Let me spin whatever plays out!* Sydney fought the urge in her to pull her weapon and blast her way out. Instead, she turned her head back to Nikolav, her left hand sliding under the gurney.

A lump of doubt settled in the back of her throat.

Nikolav smiled at her. "You should get that wheel fixed." He chuckled. "Maybe I could help you with it. I think I have something for it back in my office."

His eyes told Sydney everything she needed to know. The man didn't suspect her at all. He was after some tail.

"Maybe next time," Sydney said with just enough sarcasm to let him know it would never happen.

The man shrugged and then hit the button at his podium. The doors opened for Sydney and her gurney.

"You've been nothing but helpful," Sydney yelled over her shoulder as she pushed the gurney and its precious cargo out to safety.

CHAPTER 8

Vaughn was certain that no one had followed him back to the safe house. He had purposely taken streets lined with storefront windows—a trick that had saved his life more then once in the field. The window's reflections helped him track the positions of people in every direction.

Not that he'd expected to be followed. He had simply reverted to old habits. He remembered an article about football players that reported a particularly high percentage of off-field altercations. The article illustrated how some players had a tough time being conditioned to tackle and destroy anything that got in their way on the ten yard line, and then turn off that part of the brain the moment they exited the field. It was a similar battle for law enforcement agents.

Vaughn found it increasingly difficult to trust others. On top of that, he felt that he needed to push even harder to make himself worthy of other people's trust. He needed to show that his intentions were true. This is why his clashes with Sydney damaged him so greatly.

More than anything, he wanted to prove that he was a different person off duty and could healthily compartmentalize the work part of his life. His best friend, Eric Weiss, was fundamentally better at this than he was. Weiss could walk back into the subway from APO and just be a guy waiting for the train home. Weiss could also walk also back into the whitewashed secret headquarters and be ready to assemble a strike force in four minutes. Vaughn allowed himself a joke. *Now, if Weiss could just lose his fondness for magic long enough to get a date, he'd be the perfect agent.* At the end of the day, he just wished both he and Sydney could be in a place to set all weapons of the job down and just . . . be.

Pulling his mind back to the duties at hand, Vaughn entered the Embargo Hotel. It was a building that had lived through many incarnations since being constructed more than a hundred years before. It had been a hotel, an apartment complex, office space, a bank, and then back to a hotel. For this reason, the hotel had numerous modern amenities, but the erratic floor plan left something to be desired. The halls weaved randomly, and there seemed to be several more staircases than necessary. Then again, it was for these quirks that APO had chosen the Embargo as a safe house location. Multiple exit strategies prove most useful when you're trying to remain covert.

Vaughn walked down the hotel corridor to their base of operations. He knew Jack and Dixon were currently away performing other tasks and hoped that there could be a private opportunity to smooth things over with the woman he cared for so deeply.

He knocked once outside suite 922. Waiting a beat, he rapped twice more in quick succession. It was the designated code. From inside, Sydney unlocked the door.

Marshall, the genius that he is, had provided an instant security system. Small wires ran to all the exit doors and windows, connected to a central laptop that monitored their surroundings. The program overrode the usual key card entry system of modern hotel rooms. Comings and goings were decided by the whim of the laptop's controller.

The comforting scent of garlic wafted from the paper bag Vaughn carried, filling the small hotel suite with something more savory than its musty upholstery and decades worth of cigarette smoke.

The receptionist at the front desk had referred to their current digs as one of their most opulent suites. This was a grand overstatement on the hotel management's part. The suite contained two small rooms: a lounge that had been converted to their base of operations and a bedroom with two double beds. A small bathroom with two entrances linked the rooms.

It was nothing fancy, but at the end of the day, Vaughn recognized that this wasn't a weekend getaway to Santa Barbara. This was work, and he had stayed in far worse. Anything with indoor plumbing was all right by him.

Vaughn set the food down on an end table. Sydney was working on her laptop and made no gesture to welcome him. He knew she was still upset by his decision to drug Faina in the mortuary. But he confidently felt he had made the right choice based on the circumstances. Otherwise, they might not have all made it out.

Hard choices and split-second decision making was part of being a good agent. Sometimes, the "nice thing" was the choice that allowed the enemy enough time to put you in their sights. Jack Bristow had taught him that time and time again. Sometimes the right choice was ugly or unfair—but it was still the right choice. If Faina felt upset, he was sorry. But the added chance of capture was not an acceptable option for him. He had done the best he could to protect everyone.

Vaughn decided to test the waters. "Dixon is disposing of the van. He should be back shortly," he said. His words hung in the air for a few moments.

"Great," Sydney mumbled, not even looking up from the keyboard as she typed. Her tone told him that the water was shallow and he better not think of diving in.

Emboldened, Vaughn tried again. "How's the girl?"

Sydney stopped typing and took a deep breath.

There was still no eye contact. "If you listen," she said, "I'm sure you'll hear the results of your exit plan, Michael."

There it was. Vaughn had learned that the use of his first name for emphasis only came in two forms. Its current form was to make him feel like a snotty schoolboy, and its other was a term of endearment that would make him melt. Currently, Michael Vaughn felt like dry ice.

With a furrowed brow he began to speak, but he was cut short by the sound of a young girl violently vomiting. He looked in the direction of the small bathroom.

"Is she going to be all right?" he asked.

Sydney looked up and met Vaughn's eyes for the first time since he entered the room. "I guess I should be asking you."

Vaughn's words jumped back at her. "It's what needed to be done in order to save our lives." He felt bad about Faina's nausea, but he was not going to apologize for securing the situation.

Silently Sydney rose, keeping her eyes on his. "I'm going to check on her," she said.

And with that, Sydney pressed past him, signaling the end of the conversation.

* * *

Sydney entered the bathroom as quietly as possible. She closed the door behind her, less for Faina's privacy than to separate herself from Vaughn.

Faina, still woozy and sick from the chemicals, kneeled on the cracked tile floor. Her head rested on her arms as she pitifully hugged the toilet bowl. In the glow of the sconces above them, Sydney could see how pale and frightened the poor girl looked. It was clear she had also been crying. Sydney offered a soothing, "Hey."

Faina wiped away the gathered tears with her shirtsleeve. Her eyes were puffy. She looked so frail, shivers wracking her small frame. *No doubt the aftermath of the cocktail of chemicals that Vaughn had forced on her.* Sydney wanted to hold her and assure her that everything was going to be okay, but she couldn't. Faina didn't turn to meet her gaze; she uttered a low groan.

Sydney crouched down next to Faina. Her objective was to be as comforting as possible, but the truth that Faina had yet to face brought Sydney pain. *How can I break this girl's heart?*

"I imagine that you're probably not in the mood for it, but Vaughn brought back some of the best

Italian food Prague has to offer." Sydney's tone sold this as a joke, and she was relieved to see that Faina at least gave her a courtesy smile.

"I'm starving, but food is sort of the last thing on my mind," Faina said, pulling herself into a sitting position on the floor. Then she added, "Thank you." The last words came out dipped lightly in cynicism, but the smile that Faina gave Sydney revealed a more subtle meaning.

Sydney looked at her in silence. She wanted to help her, not add to her grief.

"Thank you for getting me out of there."

Sydney took this in. It was said honestly, plainly, and again with a slight smile. Either Faina's nausea was fading, or her sheer determination helped her focus.

"Did you find my parents yet?" Faina asked.

"We're still working on that," Sydney said, uncomfortable with the half-truth. "We have many good agents gathering—"

Faina interrupted. "My father was obviously moved. What about my mother?"

Sydney hoped her face didn't betray the awful secret she held. But maybe her silence said enough. The girl pressed her for more information. "I need to speak with my mother. Do you have any leads? Any ideas?"

Sydney tried as best she could not to cringe at that word: *mother.* The word was still painful for Sydney to hear for her own reasons.

Faina seemed not to notice. "If you could give her a message for me . . . let her know I'm sorry. It was stupid and unimportant."

Holding back tears was becoming nearly impossible even for the seasoned agent. Sydney's chest ached with the fear of what might be coming next. But before any more emotions could unravel, the bathroom door opened.

Jack Bristow, per usual, was all business. "Sydney, I need to speak with you." Jack noted Faina, his cheek muscles barely shifting in a grimace of acknowledgment. This was the closest thing he'd define as a smile. "Now, please."

Sydney looked at Faina as Jack slipped out of the door frame. "Can I get you some water, at least?"

"No, I just want to stay close to my *friend* here," Faina said, tapping the top of the toilet seat with her knuckles. Faina put her head back down. Sydney smiled at the girl's quip and squeezed

Faina's hand. It was clammy. Faina looked like she needed a few more minutes to herself. In all honesty, Sydney needed time as well to figure out how to approach the sensitive information she knew about the girl's mother.

Then, just as Sydney stood and opened the door, Faina spoke. "You have any video games on that thing?"

Sydney turned and looked curiously at her. Faina pointed to the PDA that was peeking from Sydney's pocket. Sydney retrieved the minicomputer and used the stylus to find games of solitaire and chess. *Whatever gives her comfort.*

Handing the PDA to Faina, Sydney reminded her, "I'm just out here, if you need me."

Jack was waiting for Sydney in the lounge, and as usual, he got right to the point. "We need to move her to a more secure location."

Sydney shook her head. "Soon. But right now she's too traumatized for—"

"All the more reason to get her to a safe place," Jack said.

"No. I have a gut feeling there's more she's not telling us, perhaps unknowingly," Sydney admitted.

"We should debrief her as soon as possible."

Jack nodded. "I'll start on it now, then."

Sydney stepped between him and the bath-room door. "*I'll* question her."

Jack looked coolly at his daughter. She returned his stare. Her determination was non-negotiable.

Vaughn was quietly watching the scene play out as he pretended to be engrossed in typing an update to APO on the laptop.

Glancing now at the still-closed bathroom door, Sydney spoke to Jack in a low, intense voice. "Sorokin's daughter has been through so much already . . ."

"Sydney," her father said calmly, "I realize you want to protect this girl. But you know as well as I do that the best way to do that is to remove her as far as possible from the events of the next twenty-four hours."

Sydney started to open her mouth, but then instead of debating, she sighed. Crossing her arms, she conceded the truth. "You're right."

Truth be told, Jack looked a little surprised that she agreed with him. Their relationship had been rocky at best the past few months. As stoic as he was, it was still a slight joy to hear his daughter siding with him on any topic.

"But," Sydney said in a tone so coldly similar to her father's that it made her wince, "I'll be the one who talks with her."

Jack nodded his consent but decided to test her commitment. He stepped right up to the bathroom door, implying heavily that the girl's questioning would be best dealt with now.

Sydney took a deep breath and opened the door. She had a speech in mind, but she was not prepared for what she saw.

Faina was gone.

CHAPTER 9

Sydney expected to find Faina huddled sick over the toilet or sitting on the floor feeling better, perhaps distracting herself with the electronic games from the loaned PDA. Instead, Faina and the PDA had vanished. Sydney eyed the alternate door that led into the bedroom, knowing it had been securely locked from the outside. But now she saw a piece of wire left in the keyhole and reached out to test the door. It easily swung open. Sydney and Jack darted through into the bedroom and found Faina desperately trying to pick the lock of a door to an adjoining suite. *Why didn't Marshall's security measures alert us of the breach?*

Sydney took Faina by the shoulders as gently as she could. Faina hardly struggled. She knew she was caught.

Jack noticed that one of the security wires had been bisected. And Sydney's PDA was sitting on the bedroom's window ledge, its white plastic casing stripped back, leaving its copper innards exposed. *Not every person in the world can do that, let alone a seventeen-year-old kid.*

A wire was sticking out of Sydney's PDA, and the on-screen number patterns were rotating. *What the hell is that thing?* The second question, and perhaps more important to Jack Bristow, was, *Who are we dealing with?*

Once Sydney brought Faina back into the lounge, the girl started to struggle wildly.

"Get your goddamned hands off me!" she screamed.

Sydney brought her face close to the frightened girl's.

"Faina—"

"Leave me—"

"Calm down," Sydney said. Vaughn started to

move toward them to help, but both Sydney and Faina delivered a simultaneous look that said they wanted nothing to do with his methods of control.

Still struggling with Faina, Sydney again tried to calm her down. "Listen to me! We found you. Doesn't that register that we're here to help?"

"We're doing everything in our power to find your father," Jack said, immediately realizing his mistake.

Faina stopped struggling.

The look on Faina's face told Jack that she was analyzing his words and their latent implications. It wasn't what Jack had said, but what he *hadn't* said.

Faina looked plaintively at Sydney. "My mother's dead, isn't she?"

"Work, damn it," were Weiss's encouraging words to the fax machine. "We've got control of satellites that can pinpoint a golf ball in another hemisphere, but we can't get a decent fax machine."

As Weiss raised his arm to give the object of his frustration a little slap, Marshall Flinkman came bouncing in, annoyingly chipper in the face of Weiss's dilemma. Upon seeing Marshall enter the room,

Weiss lowered his hand. He recalled the last time Marshall saw him abuse a piece of electronics. He earned a button with the slogan ROBOTS NEED LOVE TOO.

"We need interns," Weiss proposed. "At the CIA we had a bunch of eager beavers able to do all sorts of mundane tasks." Championing laziness, like only Weiss could, brought up nostalgic feelings. "Those were the glory days."

Weiss wrapped up his little daydream to focus on Marshall's raised index finger. "If we're part of a secret organization, how are we going to have interns?"

Weiss was preparing a rebuttal when Marshall's cell phone rang.

"Flinkman phone," Marshall answered. "If you need thinkin', you need Flinkman—"

"Marshall," replied Jack Bristow's cold voice, "how competent do you have to be to bypass the security system you sent with Sydney?"

All Marshall could say was, "Is it April Fool's? No one could bypass my syst—"

"I'm serious, and I want to know everything about Sorokin's daughter, Faina."

"O—," was all Marshall could sputter before Jack disconnected.

Marshall, still holding the phone to his ear, noticed Weiss's inquiring eyes, and for a second he wondered if he should try and play off that he hadn't been hung up on by Jack Bristow. He decided it was simply best to get on with his work, and he left Weiss to his own devices with a small wave of his left hand.

Weiss watched Marshall leave. *He may be a genius, but man, I wish I knew what planet he was from.*

With a shrug Weiss turned back to the fax machine, but he spun around when Marshall popped his head back in.

"I'm allergic to animals, actually the dander that animals give off, thus all things machine are my pets," said Marshall. "I wouldn't hit your pooch. Don't hit my fax." With that, Marshall left him.

Weiss smiled to himself. *Now there are two things I want to hit.*

Eyeing the jammed fax machine, he again felt the presence of someone behind him. He thought it was Marshall and spun around. "A fax is nothing like a dog!"

He realized Nadia was standing before him. She wore a troubled look on her face, but even a mountain of despair couldn't hide the fact that she was the most beautiful thing he had ever seen. He stammered, "I . . . I thought that—"

"Don't worry about it," Nadia added with a short smile. "It's not been an easy night for any of us."

Weiss stood there awkwardly. It was as if they were in high school and he wanted to invite her to the big dance three days away. Weiss snapped himself out of his delusions. "You need help with something?"

Nadia looked down at the file in her hand. "It's stupid, but could you bring this file to Sloane for me? I'm trying to stay focused, and if I see him right now, I fear I might lose some of that."

Weiss would have walked off a building if she'd asked him. He put out his hand for the file but kept his eyes on her perfect brown ones. "Of course," he added as he took the file from her.

Nadia dipped her head to say thank you and turned to get back to the time-sensitive work at hand.

"Nadia?"

She stopped and turned. Weiss could tell there was something on her mind, but they both knew that their friends and family were in the field counting on them. With so much that could be said, he summarized the subtext as best he could in a few sentences. "Things get complicated in life. But I've seen you weave through worse. . . ." She waited for more, and he had but one final thought to give. "Do what's going to make you happy."

His kind words registered on her face. And in turn, it made him warm to make her feel better. Surprised with himself that he didn't put his foot in his mouth, he decided that for once he'd stop while he was on top. "I'll see you later," he said. He drank in her features for one more second and then went back to loathing the fax machine.

Faina preferred the bedroom dimly lit, as if she could keep her tears at bay in the dark. Sydney had volunteered to keep watch, taking a seat on the double bed across from the puffy-eyed girl. What ate away at Sydney's core was that she could easily place herself in Faina's shoes. Betrayal, guilt, worry, hope, and determination were emotions her life too had been filled with. It killed her to watch Faina suffer as she herself had.

Faina looked so lost and alone.

Where was she going when I caught her?

But Sydney also saw strength in Faina. When they had briefed her with what they knew about her family's abduction, she asked questions rationally. She seemed focused.

Unfortunately, along with the strength, Sydney saw burden in Faina's face. Her mother was on Faina's mind; not just her loss, but the realization of how they had parted. Sydney was reminded of all the things she and her own mother didn't get to resolve—*both* times she lost her.

Sydney spoke softly, the way she wished someone had spoken to her when she was the lost little girl. "I have something for you." Sydney produced Anna's cameo necklace, offering it to Faina. Faina's eyes opened wide in recognition, almost hesitant to believe the sight was true. Sydney understood her reaction all too well. "I lost my mother too, when I was young."

Taking the cameo in her hand, Faina caressed the locket with her thumb. She traced the grooves of its cover as if it were a record, as if they would somehow play the memories of her mother back to her. Her head was down, and this was the first time all night that she appeared much younger then she actually was. Through her scrapes and vehement protests, Faina came off as a young adult, opinionated and strong. Now, at her most wounded, she seemed to have a childlike innocence and vulnerability. Mostly she appeared to be paging through the photo album that every person held in his or her head.

Sydney tried to offer some form of personal condolence.

"When my mother died, I was left with very few things that were hers. Over time I realized how lucky I was. The items mattered less. I had what was important—her memory. She lives within me." The words were painful for Sydney to verbalize. After all, Sydney's mother was an enigma in so many ways. Irina's intentions stemmed from a mix of vile deeds and mysterious love, a love whose nature her daughter still had no concrete proof of.

Sydney paused, testing whether to continue. There was something else she wanted to know. "What was the drawing?" she asked, referring to the inside of the cameo. "Did you make that for her?"

There was a long pause.

Just when Sydney thought silence would be the only thing the two shared, Faina offered an explanation. "I made the drawing when I was four. My parents liked to go to the museum. That's where they met. Anyhow, I didn't want them to go one day. They were leaving me with a sitter." Faina smiled at her unfolding memory. "So I made my own art for my mom to look at so she wouldn't need to leave." She wiped away a teardrop, then continued. "She and my dad had a big laugh—which I didn't get at the time, . . . She gave me a big hug and said that I was their muse and that she'd keep it with her forever."

Faina started silently crying again, tears trailing down her face.

Sydney looked up to see Vaughn standing in the doorway. His arms were crossed, but his body language wasn't cold; he was simply expressing that he was just there to check on them.

Sydney reached out to comfort Faina. But as her hand touched Faina's, Faina jerked hers away.

"Don't touch me," said Faina, wiping her nose with the back of her hand.

Sydney recoiled. "I'm sorry."

"I will find the man who did this and kill him!" said Faina, her voice rising.

Sydney tried to preempt Faina's meltdown. "You're upset—"

Faina laughed mockingly, "God, what else do you want me to be? Pushov's out there right now and we're doing nothing!"

"I know you've lost so much," Sydney tried yet again, but Faina was caught in her own momentum.

"These tears aren't for loss; they're for blood. He found me, I'm sure I can find him!"

Sydney shot Vaughn a look that screamed, *What the hell does that mean?* Sydney tried to find the right words. "I know you've been through a lot today, but there are other answers—"

"You're right to want them dead," said Vaughn matter-of-factly.

The directness of his language silenced both Sydney and Faina. Faina's face showed interest, and a little disbelief that someone was actually siding with her. Sydney, on the other hand, was dumbstruck by Vaughn's audacity.

If Vaughn noticed, he didn't show it. "I know that feeling—the betrayal, the need to correct things. . . ." Sydney knew he was speaking from experience. But she could hardly understand how Vaughn's hate would help Faina in any way.

"And you're right," Vaughn continued, "those responsible should suffer. They'll pay." With that, Vaughn left the room, avoiding Sydney's eyes.

Sydney turned to calm Faina but found the girl oddly satisfied by his remarks. Faina's face no longer glistened with anger. Rather, she appeared focused. Sydney viewed the young woman across from her as a shattered mirror. Vaughn may have scooped some of the pieces together, but that in no way made her whole again.

"Are you trying to ruin that girl's life?"

Sydney confronted Vaughn in the lounge area. Her body language was as easy to read as a freeway billboard. Her eyes looked up at Vaughn's, disapproval registering across all levels.

Vaughn realized how inane his "How's Faina?" inquiry was the moment he said it.

Sydney couldn't believe him, the irony of his remarks. In the second of waiting for her response, Vaughn began to construct protective walls around his emotions. He knew what force, like a tornado in the distance, was coming. Sydney's next words were deliberate, delivered like an advancing swordsman but with ammunition not just pulled from the adjacent room.

"You sit in my home. You charm me," Sydney said. "You implore me to believe. . . . And the worst of it, Michael? I believed you!"

"Syd . . ."

"I felt like you were opening up to me when you told me that you wanted to change. Maybe . . . maybe you're incapable of it." Their past was complicated; they both knew that, but the past few weeks had been a dance between hope and failure. They both knew it had the potential to consume them if they did not find some resolve.

Vaughn wanted more than anything to be with Sydney, and he genuinely felt the same pull from her. The problem wasn't the desire to be together, it was the actual application of it. The question still remained, *Would they be able to unite before their differences made it all fade away?*

"What's consuming you, Michael? You used to risk your life to protect innocents just like Faina. I refuse to believe that the Michael Vaughn I know has given that up."

He couldn't sit silent anymore. *I made the hard choice.* He had his own take on what happened in that basement, and hoping she'd understand, he laid it out for her. "Nothing consumes me. I've finally seen the world for what it is. My decision in the mortuary saved us!"

"And that's what frightens me, the *justification* for your actions. You acted just like my father, seeing yourself as right. He always puts it in those terms. It either is or isn't, for him. Is life that black and white to you? Is our relationship?"

"What would you have me do, Agent Bristow?" He felt like he was being schooled. "We were running out of time. It's easy now to tell me what was right or wrong, but remember, we're *alive* right now and have the luxury of this wonderful diatribe!"

The only thing more uncomfortable than having a loved one yell at you is the silence. They were at a standoff, an unfixable juncture. An apology would simply mask the larger issue. Would what they had simply be worn down by uncontrollable forces?

Vaughn broke the standstill, trying to salvage something good. "Sydney, I'm sorry. My intent was in no way to hurt the girl. . . ." He let that lie out there for a few seconds. The room was quiet, and he stepped closer to relay the next part of his argument. "There's something more here, Sydney. Faina was hysterical, and that helps no one. If we keep her focused, maybe we have a chance of getting something that'll bring Victor to—"

"You don't understand," yelled Faina from the next room. "I can't leave!"

Jack.

Their personal life on hold, Vaughn and Sydney went to investigate the drama unfolding next door.

Jack had Faina by the wrist. "We are moving you for your own safety, Miss Sorokin," he said. "And to be perfectly honest, you are not our main objective—"

"But I *was* Victor's main objective," Faina said as she whipped her hand from Jack's hold. No one could get free from Jack Bristow unless . . . unless he *wanted* them to believe they were in control. Sydney watched the scene play out. *My father always has a motive.*

"In sixteen hours your father is giving a speech. It's important to the world that's he's there," Jack said. Sydney realized he was testing Faina. Drawing her out.

"His speech isn't why Victor wants him," said Faina defiantly. "I mean it is, but—"

"Then why take him?" asked Vaughn.

"To return him . . . ," Faina said, quieter now. All eyes were on her. "Because he has access to everything."

Sydney noted the simple truth of the statement. It was starting to become clear. Sorokin's speech, not to mention his standing in the political community, gave him free reign over the conference. He was well-known in these circles. No one would suspect him as a security threat.

"You're right," Faina continued, "my father is scheduled to give a speech to an audience of very important people who collectively control the world economy. You already know this."

"Yes," Jack Bristow said. "Tell us what we don't know."

"My father was chosen . . . because of me. I have a . . ." Faina paused, trying to find the right word. "A talent." She commanded the room's full attention. "Victor threatened me. They made me do it."

"Made you do what?" Sydney asked, trying to show the girl that she was on her side. "What did they make you do?"

"Vests," Faina said, her head down and turned away. "They gave me Kevlar vests rigged with explosives." Sydney, Jack, and Vaughn felt their minds racing to connect all of the proverbial dots. The feeling in the room was electric.

Sydney recalled the Kevlar snippet and the evidence of soldering that Vaughn had found in the mortuary's basement. She watched as Vaughn produced it from his pocket and handed it to Jack. He stood nearby, waiting to see what Jack's assessment was.

Jack Bristow was always wary of the presumed ordinary. He was his own best example. A man in a suit, was how he came across in video surveillance or walking down the street. He could navigate a bustling avenue in Times Square and none of the thousands he'd pass would guess him to be the force that he was. Cautiously he sized up Faina.

And Sydney's own fear was forming in her mind as she realized the extent of Faina's skills. *Faina is more like me than I ever imagined.*

In a tense voice, Faina presented the grand dilemma before them, in one simple and horrifying revelation. "They made me write and install a program that allows my father to pass through any form of electronic security. Victor plans to detonate what I made during the oil conference."

CHAPTER 10

"She's *Junebug*?!"

Marshall's excitement was loud and clear, even over the somewhat fragmented video conferencing software that now linked the group in Prague with APO headquarters. "She's like . . . a cyber celebrity. Could you have her sign a microprocessing system or something—"

Jack Bristow interrupted the rant before it could really pick up steam. "If you're in such a fit to meet her, why are we only hearing about her now?"

"Knowing of her—wow, Miss Sorokin is

Junebug—and knowing *who* she is are two vastly different things. Per example, exhibit A." Marshall placed a four-by-four inch forensic placard with a bold, block-letter *A* in front of himself.

"Many people know me online, or as they say in certain circles, 'in the digital underground,' through various aliases and code monikers. But walking down the street, or shopping for diapers at the local megamart for little Mitchell, no one would know or even notice me." His face drained to sadness for a beat. "Kind of like high school."

Marshall snapped back to his usual upbeat self. "Taking a page from the man upstairs, an online god is most powerful when unseen." He smiled as he brought his point around full circle, tapping the placard. "Again, like exhibit A." He then discarded his little sign and nervously cleared his throat. "Can I talk to Junebug?"

With a nod from Jack, Faina's young face appeared on Marshall's monitor.

Respect resonated in Marshall's next words. "It's such an honor to meet you, Junebug . . . I mean, Miss Sorokin. Have you ever heard of Micro Cipher?"

Faina smiled mischievously as she recognized

the moniker. She smiled, nodding like one genius neurosurgeon to another. "Impressive."

Vaughn couldn't take this lovefest any longer and began to read aloud from a printed sheet of paper. "Junebug won Westinghouse and Russian National science prizes when she was only eleven and again at twelve. Then she seemed not to participate, at least legitimately, for a few years. When she would have been fourteen years old, someone took control of the electricity during the final judging hours, including the air conditioning, lights, and doors with electronic locks. This was coupled with the release of ten thousand *Phyllophaga coleoptera,* more commonly know as—"

"June bugs," Sydney said, seeing the larger picture before her.

"If I may," Marshall interjected with a raised finger. "It's an apt code name. The June bug, commonly know as the May bug, spring bug, or Japanese Beetle, lies dormant in various forms for up to three years before revealing itself in its most commonly recognizable state.

Vaughn continued reading. "Last year she declined early enrollment into several major universities in Europe and the States." Vaughn placed the sheet by his side and summarized the rest of his research. "Like Marshall says, she's pretty much a genius when it comes to mathematics and microelectronics. It appears Victor Pushov was the first to decipher Faina's other identity."

"So, explain what Faina developed for Victor," Jack asked Marshall.

"Why not just ask me?" Jack turned to see Faina with her arms crossed. "I'll tell you what you want to know."

The agents in the room turned their attention to her while Marshall tried to get Dixon to turn the webcam a little to the left for a better view.

"The simplest way to explain is through my initial experiment with the program. I wrote a code and installed it in the microprocessing chip of a digital watch. It was hidden and also provided a good power source for the small transmitter. Logistically, an undetectable field broadcasted and changed information read by the checkout scanner at a grocery store. Long story short, I made it so *any* item scanned by the cashier registered as a can of peaches."

Dixon interrupted. "How does this relate to the vests?"

"Ah, if I may be so bold as to speak on behalf

of the great Junebug," Marshall said. "The same principles could be put in place to trick metal detectors, both freestanding and handheld, into believing that nothing metallic was there to beep about." Marshall imitated an alarm noise. "*That* sound wouldn't go off. Thus, Sorokin could walk into the conference, deliver his speech, and all the while be a walking bomb. It's genius." He caught himself, feeling not right about placing terrorists in any sort of positive light. "In a Lex Luthor *evil* genius sort of way, that is."

"Thank you, Marshall." That was enough from Jack to silence him.

Sydney turned toward Faina, putting it all into perspective. "Victor wanted her all along. Faina was the primary objective, and her father, Anton Sorokin, would be the delivery system."

Faina locked eyes with Sydney. "Bingo."

Arvin Sloane next appeared on the screen. His gruff beard and reptilian eyes cut through Sydney. They always had, even when she was unaware of the level of his questionable deeds. Even from halfway around the world, he still had an effect on her.

She refused to believe her growing fear: *The man who killed my fiancé, the man who's plagued my life for so long, is to be a permanent fixture in it. There is no escaping Arvin Sloane.* It burned her to no end that every attempt to squelch his power was met with his snaking his way into more and more powerful positions.

"Team," Sloane stated both as a unifier and to show ownership, "Weiss and Nadia have pulled together further intel, giving us a good model of Victor's actions. We know now that the kidnapping is part of a covert bombing plot. History shows that Victor's MO always includes multiple targets."

And with that, the computer screen displayed black-and-white surveillance footage. Weiss narrated, "This was pulled from an attack in Lithuania in 1996. . . ."

The group watched the grainy footage of four adults, dressed in winter clothing, shake hands and climb into a chauffeured dark sedan.

"The passengers are three influential bankers and one's husband. They were involved in a deal to partner with Western manufacturing interests trying to jumpstart the Russian economy after Communism ended."

On the computer screen the sedan was entering an underground parking structure. Again Weiss narrated. "They're on their way to a meeting at a bank when—" His words were cut short as the sedan pulling up to the guard station burst into a gigantic fireball. The explosion was so powerful that the camera across the street shook violently. Windows in the neighboring building shattered, and the unfortunate guard at the entrance gate literally disintegrated.

Jack stared coolly at the footage on the computer screen. Sydney's trained eye, though, could see his subtle reaction. Her father was cold, she couldn't deny that, but she had never seen a person angrier at the evil that others inflicted on the innocent.

Dixon's face froze at the image. He had watched his wife die in a similar manner. If this were under different circumstances, Sydney believed that he would have probably left the room for a moment. She admired his strength, even in the face of such personal grief.

Vaughn and Faina shared a different look. It was one of determination. It seemed to unify them in a way that concerned Sydney. Faina seemed especially unfazed by the footage. Sydney was ready to comfort her, let her know that they would get her father back unharmed. Instead, she found the young woman nearly emotionless. Sydney felt as though she now had two Michael Vaughns to worry about.

Sloane's face again filled the screen. "This is only one of six examples we've pieced together of Victor taking out multiple targets. Given Sorokin's freedom from security tomorrow, all signs foretell the potential for massive casualties at the upcoming conference."

"Do we have any leads as to where Victor and Sorokin might be?" asked Dixon.

A thought came to Sydney. "They'll need to be close by."

Jack understood her reasoning. "Accurate estimation. We know for certain from Faina's design that Victor Pushov plans on detonating the bomb via a radio frequency. Their base of operations must be in relative proximity to the target. Marshall can work up a model using concentric circles to determine the most probable locations."

Vaughn turned to Faina. "Couldn't you have loaded a faulty program?"

"I *did*," Faina shot back. "You think I'm some monster? I'm not an idiot. I figured out pretty quickly what these people had planned. I tried supplying an Alice mirror program instead." She explained further after receiving blank looks. "You know, one that would look like the real thing but was distorted. I began loading the program into the second vest when they decided to test the first one. It obviously didn't work and they pulled a gun—"

"And threatened you?" Sydney worried out loud. Her words trying to get the girl's attention and keep her focused. *Vaughn had been right about that. The team needed her as composed as possible in the face of their impending challenge.*

"No, they needed her," Jack replied.

Faina nodded. "They threatened to harm my parents. Victor described in graphic detail the portrait he'd produce of *me,* in *their* blood." The look she then shot Vaughn told him he better not continue asking such foolish questions.

Victor Pushov gazed out of a large floor-to-ceiling window that offered a panoramic view of the city at dusk. Lights spread out before him. The world was so vibrant to Victor's eyes. It looked like a painting.

He smiled as the vision crystallized in front of him. Victor had chosen this setting, this canvas on which to put his colors. His masterpiece would elicit respect. After all, he knew that deep down, all artists wanted to be respected for what they stood for. And for Victor, it was the Russia that used to be, which he believed to be the best example of a people and their livelihood.

There was a flicker of doubt. He feared that like other artistic geniuses ahead of their time, he too might go unrecognized for his achievements until after his death. But the risk of others' lack of imagination was worth his political ideology. He would be part of a movement of change.

"Excuse me, sir."

Victor turned to face the interrupter. Updates were not uncommon, but his lieutenant's tone said that this might be something important.

"Sir, I've received news from the mortuary. The girl has been compromised."

Internally Victor was enraged, but his mind was already calculating the necessary change in plans. Nothing critical would change. His masterpiece would still be unveiled. "Get Sorokin dressed."

Fifteen minutes later Victor entered the open floor of a gutted office building. Three of his men worked on laptops, while two men stood guard, watching Anton Sorokin get dressed. Victor wanted to preview his handiwork.

Sorokin stood in black tuxedo pants, black socks, and well shined shoes. Strapped to his chest was a Kevlar vest. A white dress shirt, black jacket, and bow tie hung from a chair back. It was the most rudimentary of changing areas.

Victor greeted Sorokin with a smile. "I like your tux."

Sorokin simply stared at him, wanting to punish the vile man who had altered his life forever. Sorokin fought back his rage, fearing further loss. He had already seen the demise of his wife—his everything—and couldn't bear the thought of losing his beloved daughter as well.

Faina was all he had left.

Sorokin tried to stabilize his thoughts, but every time he thought of her, he felt like crying.

Special moments clouded his thoughts. He remembered a time, two years ago, when he had out-of-town business on his daughter's birthday. She was turning fifteen, and he was scheduled to speak on behalf of the Russian government to an Afghani company called Malik. The deal would create six thousand jobs in its first year, and almost ten thousand in additional positions in the two years following. It was too important to reschedule.

He fretted over what Faina's reaction would be. Even though he apologized and promised to give her the best gift ever that year, he was still extremely upset about missing the celebration. A father's pride, his wife used to call it. The Malik conference was a success, and Sorokin flew home the moment the meeting was over. A driver dropped him off at home at three forty-five in the morning. Faina was asleep in his office chair. Beside her were two pieces of cake and his unopened gift. She had waited to share it with him.

Victor had found the ultimate leverage: Faina.

"Anton, you are a brave man," Victor now icily reassured him. Victor regarded himself as an excellent judge of character—or rather, an excellent judge of worth. People in no way really interested him; but he looked beyond the actual person and saw what tool they could be for him. That's what made Faina such a precious discovery. The combination of the Sorokin family unit was like the art he so admired. Everything about it fit completely, perfectly. Faina had the power to make him undetectable, her father was the perfect vessel, and her mother was the best leverage of all. Anna was an expendable person who could be used as an example.

Now it was Victor's challenge to make sure that when Anton Sorokin left his care, there would be no question that he would carry out his duty. For this task Victor would have to inspire Sorokin. To fill him with passion.

"I want to tell you a story," Victor said.

"I'd rather not hear one."

Victor laughed at Sorokin's naïveté. "You don't have that luxury right now, Anton."

Sorokin knew that the madman was attempting to play him again, but he was a captive audience.

"There was a king," began Victor. "And this king desired his banquet hall to be repainted before a huge party took place. He needed the walls, the room itself, to breathe life." Victor pulled out a cigarette and put it in his mouth. "What the king needed was art."

Victor handed Sorokin the tuxedo shirt.

"The king knew of many artists in his land— numerous men who could have done the job and who desired the work. But one in particular, he was told, was the absolute best. The king's counselors explained to him that the artist's paintings made noblemen weep. Was it any surprise that the king had to have him?"

Victor gave a crooked smile to Sorokin as he lit the cigarette and exhaled smoke between them.

"The king sent for the artist, but the artist refused the commission. He would not even consider it. No price was good enough. He refused all monetary compensation. He shunned offers of land, mistresses, treasures, and even to live forever in the king's palace.

"The king grew impatient and said he would take the artist's land and home away. Still the artist refused. The king tried threats, but the artist stoically took out his own dagger and offered it to the king."

Sorokin studied Victor, wondering, despite himself, where the tale was heading. As if reading his mind, Victor handed Sorokin the tuxedo coat with a cruel smile.

"You see, the king was stumped, Anton. He needed something, but cooperation is a hard guarantee. Both parties need to have stakes." Victor paused for a moment, letting the not-so-subtle implication sink in. "The king's reputation was on the line, and the artist, hating the king and his policies, felt no need to come to his assistance. But then an ingenious thought came to the king, and he sent the artist back to his village. He then ordered his guards to arrive at the stubborn artist's home first and take the artist's most prized possession—his muse.

When the artist returned home, he found that his lover had been taken. The artist returned to the king and offered to paint the hall for free, as long as his lover was returned afterward." Victor smiled wickedly at Sorokin, letting this allegory sink in. "The artist did his best work. And I know you will do your job with no less enthusiasm."

"You okay?"

Faina looked up at Sydney's question. Her damp eyes betrayed recent, hidden crying. Nonetheless she stared back at Sydney stoically. Sydney couldn't help but imagine the young lady as one of those toy punching bags with the weighted bottoms. The girl had been emotionally knocked around over the past twenty-four hours, but still, she held herself upright. Sydney was impressed. *She is one tenacious girl.*

"I'm fine," Faina answered. "Thank you."

Sydney patted her on the forearm, turning to leave, but Faina surprised her with had her own question.

"The people you go after . . . do they ever *get away*?"

At first Sydney didn't quite know how to answer. But then she realized the only respectable answer was the truth.

"Sometimes," she said, choosing honesty. "But we're going to safely return your father. We have the best team available—"

"But even the best can make mistakes, right?"

Sydney took in Faina's query. Being human, of course agents made mistakes. No person—or agent—was accurate one hundred percent of the time.

"My mother used to tell me that decisions came from three places," the girl continued. "The fist, the mind, and the heart."

Sydney again was amazed at the intelligence of the young woman before her. Electronic mastery was one thing, but philosophy was another.

"The fist is the worst sort of decision—rash, and usually a strike in anger. The heart is always a much better choice and nearly always right, but the heart lies too. It can mask the truth with emotion. The mind makes the best decision, but unfortunately with the mind, one doesn't always get the resolve that the other two bring."

Faina clasped her mother's necklace hanging around her neck. She cupped the locket in one hand, and Sydney saw something new yet indefinable in Faina's eyes.

Sydney was about to walk out of the room when she was halted by another question from Faina. "I'm just curious, where are the decisions regarding my father made . . . fist, heart, or mind?"

Sydney turned and faced her. She had no idea how to answer.

CHAPTER 11

Anton Sorokin looked at himself in the mirror. Like wrapping dead flowers in gold leaf, the tuxedo only seemed to accentuate his sorrow.

No stranger to fine clothes and important parties, he remembered countless other times he'd dress formally for a night out. But then there was the excitement of an evening out with his wife, or at the very least, the desire to get things over with so he could return home and relax.

Now, looking at himself in his tuxedo, he missed the simple actions of trying to get his wife to be on time and Faina volunteering to adjust his bow tie. He cursed himself instantly for thinking of his loved ones again. He knew this was his Achilles' heel and Victor had the arrow.

Sorokin could barely restrain his disgust when Victor joined him in front of the mirror. Victor tugged on something sewn into the lining of one of Sorokin's sleeves. Next, in the palm of his hand, Victor revealed a small flesh-colored button connected to two wires. If Victor had not made such a grand display, Sorokin may not have even spotted the camouflaged device. Using an aerosol glue canister, Victor sprayed Sorokin's left hand and then proceeded to secure the item onto his palm. Sorokin's eyes met Victor's, desiring an explanation.

"Once you are inside the hall," Victor said, "you will take an earpiece out of your pocket. Fit it in snug. I wouldn't want you not to hear me clearly." Victor forced a smile. "If for any reason there is a problem, you'll know what to do."

Victor was clearly relishing this whole scene, breaking Sorokin's will. "I expect great things from you, Anton. Just keep your hand off of that little button until I say so. Art should be unveiled at its proper moment."

Satisfied, Victor turned to leave.

"I won't do it," Sorokin said gravely. Something deep inside him compelled him to speak.

Victor stopped. His henchmen turned to their boss, curiously awaiting his response to such insolence. Victor took his time turning to face Sorokin. It was almost casual, as if Victor had fully anticipated these little bumps in his agenda.

The blasé look on Victor's face only angered Sorokin. He switched tactics. "I want proof that my daughter won't be killed."

"You'll have to take my word for it," Victor answered.

"I'm sorry, but I don't trust sociopaths."

Victor was silent for a beat, his temper clearly raging inside. But when he spoke again, his voice was eerily calm. "Is your daughter a virgin, Anton?" Sorokin was used to saving face in the trenches of political and business warfare, but the direction of the conversation touched a raw nerve. "I ask because I have a man who works for me who loves little girls. Your beautiful daughter is a little older than his taste, but I'm sure he'd make an exception if I offered her."

Sorokin tried to ignore Victor, but the horrific images were impossible to shut out.

"Sometimes he blindfolds the girls. . . ." Anton wanted to kill him, then resurrect him for the opportunity to kill him over and over again. "But other times he enjoys relishing the wild fear in their eyes—"

"Enough!" Sorokin cried. "I'll do whatever you want. Just please, leave Faina alone." His daughter's safety was worth more than his own life.

"Comply and Faina lives—untouched. Paint the hall for your king and everything will be fine." Victor patronizingly adjusted Sorokin's bow tie. "You have the power to spare your daughter. But if you refuse again, I will make a call. She'll suffer so much . . . and I'll let her know every few hours that her agony is all your fault."

Nadia was on the phone requesting the release of records when an APO coworker handed her the latest surveillance report.

Midway through reading it, she immediately hung up the phone and rushed into Sloane's office.

Looking up from a pile of reports, Sloane was pleased to see Nadia approach his desk. But then his smile faded as he registered the grave look on Nadia's face. Whatever information she had to relay, it wasn't good.

In Prague the APO team and Faina gathered for an emergency meeting. Sloane's serious face filled the computer screen.

"I regret that the situation has changed," Sloane reported ominously.

"How so?" asked Jack.

"Our surveillance outside the conference just sighted Sorokin entering the Royal Moscow Hotel."

Faina pushed past the others to get closer to the computer. "My father, is he okay?"

Jack turned to Sydney, Vaughn, and Dixon. "The timetable must have shifted as a result of Miss Sorokin's extraction," he said, immediately absorbing the implications. "It won't play out at the conference. The bombing is rescheduled for tonight."

The Audi S8 roared through the narrow, rain-slicked streets of Prague toward the Royal Moscow Hotel.

Sydney and Vaughn were in the backseat of the vehicle with Faina wedged between them. Behind the wheel, Jack effortlessly navigated the tight cobblestone streets. Dixon sat in the passenger seat, his laptop open and plugged into the cigarette lighter. His PDA was plugged into the computer's USB port per Marshall's request.

"Okay guys," said Marshall via computer

remote, "after looking at the schematics of the bomb design—thanks for the info by the way, Junebug—I mean Faina . . ."

Faina leaned forward. "Not a problem, Merlin."

"It's really Marshall. Merlin's my code name. I know they sound similar, but—"

"Marshall," barked Jack. "Focus."

"Right. Sorry about that. Okay, we weren't planning for anything like this, so I had to simply work with what we had. I've downloaded a program into Dixon's PDA for Sydney. It's designed to push the processor housed in the Kevlar vest into a logic loop that eventually causes an overload."

"Eventually?" Vaughn asked.

"The cycle runs forty times in one eighteenth of a second. Then blammo!"

"So the PDA is going to blow up in my hand?" Sydney pointed out.

"No. It's just a processor. You won't even feel it. What it will do, however, is create an electro-magnetic pulse—a small one, but it should be enough to do the trick."

"For what?" asked Dixon.

"To fry the electronics in the bomb timer." Marshall grinned at its ingenuity.

Vaughn was less convinced. "How do you know we won't just set it off?"

"Well, I don't. But if Junebug is right about the type of device it is, in *theory*, it should do the trick."

"You mean to tell me that we're basing the mission—and our *lives*—on what a seventeen-year-old remembers about a bomb she saw yesterday?" Vaughn replied.

"I know more about electronics than you'll *ever* understand," Faina said in Vaughn's face. "I worked with that equipment for a whole afternoon. I could probably build you one from memory just with parts from the electric razor you didn't use this morning!" Faina fell back into her seat, fuming.

The reality was, they had no other plan. The car roared over a rise and the Royal Moscow Hotel came into view. It was surrounded with activity in preparation for tomorrow's conference.

Jack took a mental snapshot of the surroundings.

Marshall cleared his throat. "There's one more thing I need to tell you. Actually, two things. Remember, this is as jury-rigged as you can get. I mean, I didn't even get to touch anything."

"Marshall, what is it?" Jack asked impatiently.

"You only get one chance to use the device. After it fries the processor, your gizmo won't be good for anything except a paperweight."

"And the other thing?" Sydney asked.

"We're talking about very small amounts of electricity here. Less than three volts. It has virtually no range. You'll have to be right next to Sorokin for it to work."

"Ten or fifteen feet?" Dixon asked.

Marshall shook his head. "Pipe dream. You'll need to be right next to him. In fact, touching him is best. The pulse will be more powerful."

Jack parked the Audi at the end of a discreet alley. Once he turned the lights out, the car became practically invisible in the shadows. Disengaging the key, he turned to face everyone. This was it.

Sydney began to diagram the plan. "Dixon and I will infiltrate the hotel."

Dixon commented, "Inside are countless rooms and several thousand people. How are we going to locate Sorokin before he sets off the bomb?"

Faina spoke up. "I might be able to help with that."

They all glanced at her. Her determined face seemed much older than her age.

"The basis for my stealth technology is a sort of electronic curtain," Faina continued. "If I could get to a powerful enough receiver . . ."

Dixon completed her thought. "You could locate your father and the location of any other vests."

Smiling, Faina nodded. "Using a laptop, I can hack into the hotel security systems and utilize the sonic sensors to triangulate the signal. There is one thing, though . . . the pulse device Marshall rigged will work only when my jammer is down."

"And how are we supposed to get around that?" asked Vaughn.

"You don't. It's built into the system. It's just going to take some close timing . . ."

Vaughn began to protest. "We're already behind the gun here, this sounds like—"

Faina cut him off. "When the jammer detects the desired radio signal, it automatically shuts down so that the receiver can get it. This is the only time the converted PDA will have a chance of working. I'll see the change in the signal and tell Sydney when to do it."

"What kind of time window are we talking about?" asked Jack.

"Five seconds," replied Faina.

Before Vaughn had a chance to object, Sydney expounded on her original plan. "Okay, Faina and Vaughn will locate and track Sorokin's vest. Dixon and I will then get to your father and wait. When you give me the word, I'll do it. Any questions?"

No one said a word. There was no time left for debate.

"All right," Jack said. "Vaughn, take Faina to the back of the hotel. For a conference this important there will be media equipment setting up for tomorrow." He opened his door. Sydney stopped him. "And you?"

Jack looked at his daughter. "I'm going to find Victor and the rest of those vests." With that, Jack headed for the buildings across from the hotel with his cell phone to his ear.

Vaughn turned to Sydney, his deep eyes more expressive than words. "It goes without saying, but—"

"I'll be careful," Sydney said, touched by his concern. "I promise."

Dixon cleared his throat. "Let's go."

APO headquarters was abuzz with activity. All present had only one focus—to try to minimize the potential catastrophe unfolding in Prague. Nadia and Marshall were at the center of the organized chaos.

Window after window opened and closed on Marshall's computer screen as he frantically typed. He could barely keep up with Nadia's requests.

Just then a small window in the bottom right corner of Marshall's screen appeared, indicating an incoming message. Jack's steely voice came over the speakers. He got right to the point. "I need a breakdown of the area around the main ballroom of the Royal Moscow Hotel. Specifically, I want to target any buildings that could be used to beam a high density signal into the ballroom."

"I'm on it."

"And Marshall? I need that information *now.*"

The lobby of the opulent Royal Moscow Hotel was crammed with guests and their designer luggage. But to the trained eyes of the couple sitting on an emerald velvet banquette, the hotel was also overrun with uniformed and plainclothes security.

Sydney brought the magazine she was pretending to be engrossed in close to her face. "Security is tight."

Dixon spoke low to her. From a distance they

looked like weary travel companions suffering from jet lag. "I count ten. How about you?"

Turning her head as inconspicuously as possible, Sydney counted them off. "Okay, four covering the main entrance, two inside and two out. One by the concierge desk, two manning the metal detector near the bellboy station, obviously checking bags. And three stationed around the front desk."

"What's our plan? We're not going to be able to sit here indefinitely, waiting for Sorokin to appear."

Sydney watched a businessman carry his garment bag through the metal detector. "I've got an idea." She stood and whispered in Dixon's ear, "I'll be right back."

Sydney entered the hotel gift shop. Two minutes later she returned with a shopping bag.

Dixon glanced inside the bag to find that it contained half a dozen large bars of milk chocolate, a red plastic squirt gun, and the tackiest-looking guidebook to Prague she could find.

"Quite a collection of souvenirs," he joked.

"Open the chocolate. We need the foil."

As inconspicuously as possible, Dixon peeled the candy from its wrappings, being careful to avoid tearing the foil. Sydney prepared the squirt gun. The toy was smaller than an actual weapon, but its shape was convincing. Discreetly she got to work.

Five minutes later the toy was completely coated in multiple layers of foil. Pleased with her work, Sydney snapped off a small piece of the discarded chocolate and popped it in her mouth.

Just then a wealthy couple exited the elevator bank and approached the concierge desk. The man was in his late forties with a decent build. His companion, a woman in her early twenties, seemed a compatible size.

Perfect.

In the rear parking lot of the Royal Moscow Hotel, Vaughn and Faina slowly made their way through a maze of limos, sedans, and news trucks with their own portable generators. A French news van near the edge of the parking lot felt like a perfect spot to set up shop.

"This looks good. There's no one around and it's out of the way," Vaughn assessed quickly.

"So how are we going to do it?" Faina asked.

"*We're* not doing anything. Wait here. I'll be back in a second."

After some crafty lock picking, Vaughn stealthily

slipped inside the back door of the news truck. The interior was completely dark except for the glow of a bank of monitors. At the control room deck Vaughn discovered he was not alone. A half-awake technician was reviewing some archival footage of the previous conference. As Vaughn crept closer, he reached into his pocket and pulled out what looked like an aerosol mace can.

One close-range burst of knockout gas later, the technician was slumped over his control panel. Vaughn went to work binding the technician's hands and feet with electrical tape. A soft footstep caused him to spin around.

Faina was standing in the doorway. She couldn't resist saying, "I'm surprised you didn't poison him with some ether."

"I've got it!" Marshall cried. "I've narrowed it down to three buildings: the People's Bank across the street, the Foreign Ministry behind and one block south, or the Oskarhurst Building next door."

Jack was calling from a street corner across from the Royal Moscow Hotel. "We can eliminate the Foreign Ministry building. Of the three, it is by far the most publicly secure and thus unlikely to be

Victor's chosen location. Merlin, I need more information. I only get one crack at this."

Marshall frantically searched multiple databases looking for any hint that might help them.

"Raptor, this is Evergreen. It's the Oskarhurst. I'm sure of it!"

Marshall could hear Prague's street noise as Jack began making his way toward that building. "Evergreen, what makes you so sure?"

Back at APO, Nadia scanned the incoming data on her terminal as she spoke. "The People's Bank has a security system at least as sophisticated as the Ministry and no record of new tenants in the past three years. The Oskarhurst, on the other hand, is an old office building in the midst of being converted to lofts. It has to be the one."

Jack paused, and then drew the same conclusion. "I'm on my way in. Good work."

As Jack disconnected, Nadia looked at Marshall to discover him giving her a double thumbs-up.

"Whoa," he said. "Jack gave you a compliment. That's like Halley's Comet rare."

Nadia smiled back at him, and then something caught her eye. Looking up, she saw Sloane watching her from his office. She froze for a moment, returned his tentative smile, then rushed back to her own workstation.

Sydney looked up from her guidebook to see Dixon waiting for his turn at the metal detector. He was third in line behind two businessmen and their mountain of luggage. He knelt to retie his shoes. She watched him stand and put his right hand in his pocket—that was the signal!

Nonchalantly Sydney pulled her cell phone from her pocket and speed-dialed a number. Across the room she heard a cell phone ring. Dixon as well as the two businessmen pulled out their phones. He left the line to take the call.

Hanging up and putting the phone back in her pocket, Sydney turned to the concierge desk. The wealthy couple stood there arguing about where to have dinner. Sydney made her way over to the concierge desk and stood directly behind them.

"Didn't we eat there last night?" the man asked his wife. She shrugged indifferently as she opened her clutch purse. There, buried among various makeup products, Sydney spotted a hotel key card.

Well that's easier than pickpocketing.

It was then that Sydney heard the alarm of the

metal detector chirp behind her. Everyone in the lobby, including the wealthy couple, turned to the commotion. As Sydney moved to get a better look she bumped the woman's purse, spilling its contents onto the floor.

Apologizing, Sydney dropped to the ground to gather the contents of the bag. "I'm so clumsy," she said. The woman smiled but seemed more interested in the spectacle at the metal detector.

Handing the purse back to its owner, Sydney apologized once more and then walked away from the chaos of the lobby. Walking past Dixon, Sydney smiled and flashed the woman's penthouse hotel room key.

CHAPTER 13

Victor took in the city's lights. Rain gave the city a crisp clarity that never seemed to last long enough. *Soon I will apply myself to you,* he swore. *From a palette that no one else has the courage to paint from.*

The sound of a throat clearing summoned his attention. Without turning from the view, he answered, "Yes?"

"Sir, we just received an updated report regarding the girl's escape."

"And?"

"She didn't do it alone."

Victor faced his lieutenant, his anger building. The lieutenant handed him a file of black-and-white surveillance stills.

As Victor rifled through the digital photos, his lieutenant offered more explanation. "Someone took control of the camera system, looping old footage, so we—"

Victor grew impatient. "Get to it."

The injured guards described a woman. The only available shot that matched the description was of a visiting medical examiner on the ground level."

Victor flipped through the photos until he found the image of the mysterious intruder. The lieutenant pointed to the image. "I took the liberty of having Mikhail clean up the best image we had."

Victor studied the last photograph, staring at the clear face of Sydney Bristow.

Walking through the entrance, Jack saw only one person in the lobby of the Oskarhurst Building. A young-looking doorman sat in a folding chair next to a makeshift security desk. It was obvious that Jack would not be able to slip past him unseen.

Oh, well.

The doorman looked up as Jack nonchalantly marched past his station and walked directly to the elevator bank.

Jack pushed the elevators' call button. The flustered doorman, vainly attempting to straighten his rumpled jacket, ran to catch up to him.

"Pardon me, sir, but I'm afraid all guests must be announced," he said in his most official voice.

Jack looked past the man, surveying the unfinished security station. *About what I expected,* he thought, noting the bare wires and gaping holes where the video monitors and communication equipment had not yet been installed.

"And who do you think you will call?" Jack said, his intense stare daring the doorman to further delay him. "The unit hasn't even been completed yet."

The doorman's confidence wavered, but he did not retreat.

Pushing the call button again, Jack gave him an exasperated look. "I really don't have time for this. I will only be up there for a moment." Just then the doors parted and Jack attempted to step in. But with surprising agility, the guard inserted himself between Jack and the open elevator.

"I'm sorry, sir, but I *will* need to contact some-one before I can let you up."

I don't have time for this. . . .

The bothersome doorman had no idea how lucky he was that the lobby's wide windows made it easily visible from the busy street outside. It was too risky for Jack to simply incapacitate the doorman. He would have to perform a more subtle power maneuver.

The doorman began looking through his procedure book, trying to find an appropriate number to call.

Jack made his move.

"My name is Rothenstein," said Jack, using the most condescending tone possible. "And be sure to tell whomever it is you speak to that I am going up to unit twelve-eighteen so that I can prepare the final designs for its new tenants. And since it appears I will be late for my meeting with the new tenants in exactly . . . ," Jack looked down at his watch, ". . . four minutes, I will need your name to tell them who was personally responsible for my delay."

The doorman froze with indecision.

Playing the role to the edge, Jack got in the

doorman's face. "Well, come on, man. Do you think I have all night? Make your call if you must."

The doorman's eyes darted with doubt. "I apologize. I am new to this job. Please head up to the unit. I will clear it with my supervisor when he comes in."

"Very good," replied Jack as he returned to the elevator. He pushed the call button again.

The elevator doors slid open with a *ding*, and Jack went in. In case the doorman had already changed his mind, Jack was more than ready to yank him into the elevator.

"If you will excuse me for asking," said the flustered doorman, "I hope you will let this unfortunate incident remain unreported."

Pushing the button for the penthouse, Jack turned to the doorman.

"Let's forget I was even here."

"Thank you, sir."

Jack offered the faintest of smiles as the doors slid shut.

Faina sat at the news truck's console, testing the controls. Beside her, Vaughn pulled his laptop out of its case and began connecting assorted cables. Faina looked up from her examination of the multitude of switches in front of her and grabbed a power source plug and a FireWire cable. She pointed to the truck's computer servers. "The jacks for the computer should be on a panel over there."

Vaughn hooked the laptop into the satellite truck's interfaces. Once satisfied, he pulled out his cell phone and dialed APO headquarters.

"I'm here," Marshall answered. Vaughn could hear him frantically typing in the background. "And I'm connected to your computer . . . now."

The screen on Vaughn's laptop lit up with a photo of Marshall's boy, Mitchell, in the lower right-hand quarter.

"Is that your little boy?" Faina asked.

"Yeah. I know it's not very professional, but I usually don't use this interface for work and he is so cu—"

"Less baby, more setup," Vaughn said.

Faina rolled her eyes.

"Um . . . these are the settings you'll need to change," Marshall replied. Mitchell's photo disappeared from the screen and was replaced by four sets of coordinates, each one for a separate antenna on the truck. "Don't worry, we'll be online before you can say Junebug."

* * *

The elevator doors opened on the penthouse floor at the Royal Moscow Hotel. Sydney saw exactly what guests were rewarded with when opting for the high-priced suites. Before her was a large circular greeting room with a fountain in the center. The sculpted marble fountain was a casting of four winged cherubs endlessly spitting water into a large base surrounded by chairs, love seats, and sofas, all upholstered in an expensive, if gaudy, patterned velour.

"Classy."

"Give them a break," Dixon said. "Ten years ago this would have all been concrete gray."

The east penthouse suite, identified by a small brass placard, was to their left. But just as Sydney was about to insert the key card, they heard the voices of people approaching on the other side of the door.

There was no place to hide.

"Darling, you *promised* me the diamond bracelet," Sydney said in her poutiest Southern accent, as the room door opened to reveal two uniformed maids pushing a linen cart. "You know I only like the extra sparkly ones."

"Sparkly?" Dixon said, instantly falling into the character of a wealthy Southern businessman.

"No jewel is gonna shine brighter than your eyes, buttercup."

Sydney kissed Dixon on the cheek as the two housekeepers, smirking, pushed their cart past them. With a *ding,* the elevator doors opened, and the maids pushed their cart inside. Then the doors slid shut.

The penthouse suite's decor was a curious mixture of original Old World elegance and eighties panache. Most of the suite was a huge living room with no less than half a dozen floor-to-ceiling windows offering a breathtaking view of the river and the city. A pair of French doors led to the bedroom . . . and the clothes they needed to fit in with the upscale preconference crowd.

"I hope she brought another evening dress," Dixon said.

"Dixon, she's a woman, a *rich* woman. Trust me, she'll have several options with shoes and bags to match." Sydney went to search the bedroom's closet and dressers.

"I'll check in," Dixon said, walking back into the living room. He tested the communication link. "Eagle's Nest, this is Outrigger. . . ."

There was no answer. For some reason their comms weren't working. Sydney figured it was due to the conference security measures. *Faina, you need to be as good as I know you are.*

Dixon grabbed the room phone and punched in a series of numbers to make the line secure. A second later he was on the phone with Marshall.

"We are inside and preparing for insertion."

"Copy Outrigger," Marshall answered.

"Any word from Shotgun or Raptor?"

"Both are online. When will you be ready for insertion?"

"Within five minutes."

Nadia's voice joined Marshall's. "Outrigger, this is Evergreen. We may have a problem. Earlier tonight hotel security came across what they thought was a weapon in a guest's luggage."

Dixon paused. "Yes. We heard about that. . . ."

Sydney walked through the French doors wearing a pale pink evening dress so snug that at a distance it looked painted on. She held out a tux for Dixon. She was about to say something when Dixon held up his hand, his face concentrating on the call.

Nadia continued. "The scare set everybody off. The Městská Policie wanted to close down the banquet but they were overruled. However, they set up extra security checkpoints at all the entrances. From the looks of their protocol, I don't think they're going to let the PDA in."

"What about our comms units? Will they be detected?" Dixon asked.

"No. Most of the receiver is ceramic. They shouldn't prove any problem, and the transmitter will look like dental work."

"We'll figure out another way to get everything in." Dixon gave Sydney a *we're in deeper* look. "We'll be in contact. Out."

Faina tossed Vaughn his comms set. She already had hers on.

"I was able to access the hotel's security cameras," she said as she flipped on a row of switches and the dozen or so monitors came to life, each displaying a different view of the gala going on in the hotel.

"And the sensors?" Vaughn asked, trying to mask his astonishment.

"Online in twenty seconds." Faina turned the laptop toward Vaughn. One large window was open on the screen and divided into quarters. Each one displayed what looked to Vaughn like a bunch of wildly oscillating electric signals.

"And you can read that?" It made no sense to him.

"Absolutely," she said proudly.

Electronics took time, which was the very thing this mission had in short supply.

Marshall's eyes were riveted to the screen. As he tapped the keys, the banks of monitors on the wall at APO began receiving Faina's feeds from the hotel security cameras.

"Man, Junebug is *that* good." Nadia came up behind Marshall.

Marshall's screen went black and then a nanosecond later was replaced by the same screen that Faina had on her laptop. Nadia observed the monitors. "Have we heard from Sydney?" she asked.

"We're unable to talk to her directly." Reading Nadia's look, he added, "This wasn't supposed to happen yet. We aren't prepared. We can talk with Vaughn in the truck. But as far as Sydney and Dixon are concerned, we're Big Brother. All we can do is monitor their transmissions. But Junebug—Faina—has partial contact."

But Nadia wasn't listening. On the bottom left corner monitor, a group of exquisitely dressed women approached the main entrance to the pre-conference ball.

Catching on, Marshall transferred the feed to the main screen. One of the women was Sydney.

"It's showtime."

CHAPTER 14

The ballroom was crowded with people dressed in tailored tuxedos and designer evening gowns. *Sheep to the slaughter,* thought Victor as he watched the scene play out on surveillance monitors. Behind him, half a dozen men concentrated on confirming the arrival of their assigned targets. Three more men stood at the windows, looking through high-powered binoculars to observe the myriad of vehicles driving up to the party. Photographs of particular high-profile men were included at each computer station. Once they were all assembled, Victor would make his grand artistic statement.

They had dropped Anton Sorokin off at the hotel earlier in a rented limousine. *Now that he's free—or as free as a man wearing a vest of explosives can be—can I rely on Sorokin to carry out his part of the plan?* Victor smiled at the thought. *Yes. He is like everyone else—so complacent, never considering the freedom that is to be had, the creative energy that exists outside that suffocating box called morality.*

Victor pulled out a cigarette and lit it. He turned and blew the smoke toward the window, in the direction of the hotel. *They can't even begin to comprehend how close death is to them right now.*

"I have got Birkenford in sight!" announced one of his men at the monitors.

Shaken out his musings, Victor spun back around. "Where?"

"North end, near the fireplace."

Victor watched as the main screen was switched to the observer's feed. Scanning, Victor immediately saw his first target. "Confirmed. Birkenford, Albert." Birkenford was standing between a grand piano and the huge fireplace, talking animatedly to a group of bored-looking girls. Victor smirked. "Oh please,

Albert. How many times can you tell that tiresome story? Look at those young ladies. They aren't interested in South Africa. They're interested in the *diamonds* you brought back from there."

One of the men drew an *X* across Birkenford's photograph taped to the wall. Only five other photos remained. *Albert, once your friends join you, you'll never speak of South Africa again.*

Jack cautiously stepped out of the elevator onto the twelfth floor of the Oskarhurst Building. The floor was remarkably raw and only dimly lit by a few battered yellow work lights on tripods scattered around. Stacks of drywall stood ready near the partially completed interior walls of the floor's six units, and sheets of plastic hung everywhere.

Jack's initial plan had been to go directly to the penthouse level and begin his search for Victor, but then it occurred to him that the doorman might be watching the floor indicator to see where the elevator stopped. To cover his tracks, he instead pushed the button for the twelfth floor. He'd travel by stairwell from there.

But first he pulled out his cell phone and dialed APO.

* * *

Marshall was at his computer, splitting his time between watching the hotel security monitors, checking the signal readouts from Faina, and talking to Jack.

"I don't know, Raptor," said Marshall. "It could be any of the units on that side of the building. The only criterion would be a clear view of the hotel."

That was not the answer Jack was looking for. "That's not good enough. We have to be able to narrow it down. There are still too many possible floors and units left."

Nadia and Sloane stood before the bank of monitors, watching Sydney initiate her search for Sorokin. Hearing Marshall's conversation, Nadia plugged in and asked, "Raptor, are you on the north side of the building?"

"Affirmative."

Nadia quickly searched through the electronic databases. "In your estimation, what is the lowest floor that has a line of sight to the Royal Moscow Hotel?"

Jack looked out the window at the shorter building between the Oskarhurst and the hotel.

"Best guess . . . the eighth floor."

"Okay." Nadia, and now Marshall, too, intently studied her screen. She had brought up the blueprints of the Oskarhurst Building while Marshall mathematically verified that the angle from the eighth floor would be plausible for Victor's use. "I think I can narrow it down for you," Nadia said, "by limiting the search to only the units on the north and eliminating everything below the eighth floor. I've found floors eight, nine, and ten are completely occupied, and Victor would avoid neighbors. The top two floors, fourteen and fifteen, are machinery levels, thus access would be problematic. You're on twelve, and it's empty."

"Yes, gutted."

"Then that narrows it down to either eleven or thirteen."

"And he'd want to stay as far away from any unwanted attention . . . ," said Jack, thinking aloud.

"The thirteenth floor," Nadia concurred.

"I'm on my way." Jack hung up.

Marshall held his hand out for a high five from Nadia. Smiling, she was about to slap his hand when all the monitors before them turned to static. Marshall jumped up and returned to his terminal, typing furiously.

"It's gone. The signal. It's gone!"

* * *

The Royal Moscow Hotel's grand ballroom was an incredibly huge space. Built in the thirties, it represented both the freedom and the decadence of Europe before World War II. After the Communist takeover, the hotel was used to house the occupying officers of the Soviet army, and although the official party line was that all examples of the former bourgeoisie were to be eradicated, the officers who stayed there never got around to destroying it. Perhaps they were too busy enjoying the dances on Fridays when they would invite local girls from the surrounding areas for dancing and "re-education."

Whatever the reason, after the fall of Communism the Czechs found themselves with a grand ballroom worthy of extremely formal functions, and they were sure to make use of it. Tonight, however, was an example of the downside of having a room of such huge scale. The Městská Policie had hastily set up a security checkpoint in order to prevent any unauthorized guests from entering the party. Unfortunately, the Městská Policie was dealing with a stratum of society that traditionally does not react well to any form of inconvenience. Every request to check a handbag or wave of a hand-held metal detector was met with a barrage of complaints and threats.

This was the organized chaos that Sydney walked into when she entered the section of the lobby where those waiting to enter the ballroom were assembled. Opening her handbag, she pulled out a sterling silver compact and opened it. Sitting where the makeup should be was her earpiece receiver. She deftly inserted it.

"Phoenix, this is Shotgun. Do you copy?" said Vaughn in her ear.

"Copy, Shotgun." Sydney said discreetly. "I'm preparing to head in. Dixon is working on an alternate way of getting the PDA in."

"I don't have a visual on him yet."

"Don't worry, he'll get it in," Sydney said confidently.

"Phoenix," Faina said, abruptly joining the conversation. "This is Junebug. The sensors are calibrated and online. Find my father. And remember, you'll only have a five-second window once you are in place."

The hotel's service access levels were beehives of activity. Dixon, wearing a "borrowed" workman's jacket, pushed his way up the crowded corridor toward the main kitchen. Suddenly a hand grabbed his shoulder.

"Hey, you!" said a gruff-looking man in a head waiter's coat. "I need some help here."

Using a Nigerian accent, Dixon said, "I am busy right now, but I will—"

The man shook his head. "It'll only take a minute."

Dixon reluctantly followed the man to a service bar. The head waiter stopped in front of a small printer, but that wasn't what suddenly interested Dixon.

Behind the bar was the main floor of the ballroom.

The man before Dixon looked exasperated. "This thing," he said pointing to the printer. "It stopped working. Without it we can't keep track of what we're serving. Do you know what that means?"

"It's bad?"

"You have no idea. We get paid depending on how much booze is served, and these government people drink like it's the end of the world. I know they'll try to short us if we don't keep tabs."

Dixon smiled at the man amicably. "You go. I'll fix everything."

Looking around, Sydney found what she was looking for. A group of eight young women dressed very much like her were waiting in line. Sydney shyly walked up to the group and asked, "Is this the way to get in?"

One of the girls eyed the dress Sydney had on. The girl looked about twenty going on forty-five. Her hair was raven black and her eyes deep green. Neither color, Sydney noted, was natural. The woman to her left wore an outrageously expensive midnight blue silk dress that was, impressively, even tighter than Sydney's. Sydney paid close attention to their tone, the way they spoke to one another and the way they talked about the event. Assimilation was what made a good spy a chameleon.

The woman in the silk dress commented to Sydney, "I love that color on you."

Sydney stroked the woman's ego. "It's not nearly as perfect as your dress's fit. Is that couture?"

"Yes, but who knows if I'll get to flaunt it or not. We've been in line nearly a half hour."

Assuming the same haughty attitude, Sydney said, "Why must we wait in a queue like this? I'm supposed to meet a simply perfect-looking junior member of the Dutch delegation."

Another of the girls, wearing a cleavage-baring dress, stage-whispered, "I heard there was someone with a gun here earlier."

"Really?" said Sydney.

"Yes. He pulled it out in the middle of the lobby and waved it around. Three policemen had to wrestle him to the ground."

Sydney, feigning surprise, said, "Oh my God! Was anyone hurt?"

The girls moved as the line shifted forward. Sydney stayed with them. The first girl rolled her eyes at the story.

"Don't listen to her. She watches too many James Bond movies. The police found something suspicious in one of the hotel guests' bags and of course they overreacted. Now they're checking everybody." Taking in Sydney's look of concern, she added, "Don't worry. My father is commissioner of the National Police. He wouldn't have let me near this place if there was any chance of danger."

Just then the girls reached the security checkpoint. Three officers stopped them just outside the door to the ballroom. Sydney noted, by the strained looks on the guards' faces, that they now considered the guests nothing more than people waiting to give them a hard time. One of the guards looked at the peeved woman in the blue dress and sighed. He knew this was going to be trouble.

"May I please check all your bags, ladies?" another guard asked.

Before anyone could answer, the woman in blue silk exploded in a tone only the most privileged could muster. "No! You may *not* check our bags. We've been waiting endlessly out here and for what? A toy in a suitcase? This is ridiculous!"

The first guard looked at his partner, who shrugged his shoulders. Unhooking the red velvet rope, he stepped back. "I'm sorry for the inconvenience, ladies. Please enjoy the party."

Sydney started to follow the other girls, but the guard blocked her way with a metal detector paddle. But before the guard could even say anything, Sydney's new best friend in tight couture turned to him. "She's with us! Or do you want to harass all my friends tonight?"

The officer and Sydney exchanged looks.

Sheepishly Sydney offered her open purse. He quickly glanced inside then waved her through.

"Thanks for your help," Sydney told the woman once they entered the ballroom.

"Don't worry about it. Those people need to be kept in their place and that was the perfect opportunity. Now go find your diplomat."

With a smile Sydney excused herself. Once out of sight, she dropped her guise of privileged brat. Opening her bag, she again pulled out her compact and raised it to her face. "Shotgun, I'm in. Do we have a visual on Sorokin?"

Just then a silver tray of champagne flutes was put in front of Sydney's face. Quickly she palmed the compact.

"No, thank you," she said politely in Russian.

But the champagne server refused to leave. Sydney assumed the haughty persona that worked so well against the guards earlier. "I just told you—"

But Sydney's lecture was cut short as she saw that it was Dixon dressed as a waiter. He leaned in to her. "My left jacket pocket."

Sydney reached for a champagne flute with her left hand, while her right slipped into Dixon's jacket and took the PDA.

Pretending to take a sip of bubbly from the flute, Sydney grimaced, as if to say this was not her brand of champagne. She placed the glass back on the tray and pulled her best trust fund girl out for show.

"Oh, that was awful. Please take those back to the kitchen and get something more palatable."

With a silent bow Dixon left. Holding the tray on his shoulder he spoke in a low voice as he wove his way into the crowd. "Shotgun, Phoenix is online."

The ballroom's lavish decor was filled with character and charm, and was currently occupied by the powerful and the beautiful. Sydney blended in perfectly.

In the most casual way possible, she was systematically searching from one end of the grand hall to the other as they had prearranged. Dixon was checking the far end. The plan was simple. They would both check everyone as quickly and thoroughly as possible and meet in the middle. The problem was that the population of the party was very fluid. These people were professional minglers, and consequently many of them were moving around as quickly as she and Dixon.

Then something caught Sydney's eye in the crowd. Dixon was free of his waiter garb and dressed to the nines once again.

The look in his eyes told her that he hadn't seen Sorokin either. He stepped toward her and greeted her like an old friend. "Let's switch sides," she said as they pulled away.

Nodding, he walked past her and they continued their search.

Deals have been brokered and broken at many a conference weekend. The world economy never stopped. To accommodate the participants, impromptu business centers were routinely set up in quiet corners— essentially home bases of fax machines and phones, usually manned by attractive women.

Anton Sorokin stood next in line to use its services.

"Don't be shy, now. Tell them there is an envelope for you."

Sorokin hesitated a beat, in no way enjoying Victor's voice in his ear. But with little choice, he stepped toward the attractive attendant.

"An envelope for Sorokin, Anton," he said.

The woman looked under the counter for a brief

moment and then handed Sorokin a manila envelope with his name on it.

"Open the envelope," Victor instructed.

I'm his goddamned puppet. Sorokin took out a single sheet of paper. He didn't understand its purpose. "What is this?" he asked.

"That," said Victor, in a voice that made his skin crawl, "is someone to be avoided. Your daughter's life depends on it."

Sorokin looked at the image one more time. He had no idea who this person was, nor did he care. All that concerned him was ensuring his daughter's survival. If that meant avoiding this young woman, he would do so at any cost.

He burned the image into his memory, then crumpled the picture of Sydney Bristow in his fist.

CHAPTER 15

Vaughn leaned back in his chair, staring at the monitors with his usual mask of intense reflection. *Where can Sorokin be?* It seemed that he wasn't coming, which was odd since intel indicated otherwise. Suddenly Faina gasped. Vaughn followed her gaze to the monitors and saw why.

"My father is in the ballroom. . . ."

Sydney completed her initial sweep of the floor. There was no sign of Sorokin. *Maybe they were mistaken. Maybe it* is *tomorrow.* A look of concern must have been evident on her face because the next thing she heard was, "So where is your hot Dutch diplomat?"

Turning around, Sydney came face-to-face with the leader of the earlier entourage. She handed Sydney a champagne glass.

"I just remembered I never introduced myself," the woman said, stepping back and offering a slightly tipsy curtsy. "I am Ivanna Dryosky."

Curtsying in return, Sydney replied, "And I am Anka Suoska. I'm so glad I ran into you. I wanted to thank you again."

"Oh, please." Ivanna seemed to be studying Sydney. A knowing smile developed on her face. "I bet there's another reason that you're glad to find me. I've been watching you."

Have I been made? Who is she? KGB? Městská Policie? Sydney played it cool. "Really. Have I been that interesting?" Sydney scanned the room behind Ivanna, looking for Dixon as well as the closest escape route.

The woman in blue moved closer to Sydney and then whispered in a conspiratorial tone, "You haven't been to many of these things, have you?"

Before Sydney could answer, Ivanna nudged

her with her elbow. "Don't worry. Your secret is safe with me." She drained her champagne flute. "And I bet I can guess your next question. You're wondering where your diplomat friend is."

Sydney's eyes hardened at the mention of Sorokin, but she retained the friendly tone in which they had been speaking. "*You* know where he is?" Sydney shifted her body, preparing to attack if necessary.

Misinterpreting Sydney's implication, Ivanna smiled a wolfish grin. "Don't worry, Anka. If he is what you described, I'm not interested. I like my men . . . dirtier." Ivanna took another flute off a passing tray. "He's with all the other *men of power.*"

Judging from Ivanna's derisive tone, Sydney realized her miscalculation. Ivanna had no idea who Sorokin was. But she might know *where* he— like the others of his sort—would be.

Sydney sipped her champagne. "And where is that?"

"In the library, of course. Women aren't allowed." Ivanna sighed, bored. "I was hoping that I could avoid this. Usually if one arrives late enough, they're already finished with their boys' club nonsense, but I guess that idiotic line to get in threw everything off schedule."

As if on cue, two large mahogany doors opened at one end of the hall. Men and cigar smoke flooded into the ballroom.

These sheep are so predictable! thought Victor.

"Sir! Three more of the targets have been accounted for."

Looking at the wall, Victor watched as his men drew lines through the photos of Sammick, Guyton, and Eriksson on the wall. Victor looked at his lieutenant. "Have these been confirmed?"

"Everyone at least twice. They must have all been in the library."

Victor pointed to the last remaining unmarked photograph. "And Zhursky?"

"Nothing yet."

"Well, don't take your eyes off those screens. He's the last one."

And then I can complete my masterpiece.

The fire door to the thirteenth floor was ajar, so Jack was able to enter silently. The first thing he noticed was that unlike the previous levels, this floor was completely dark. There were not even work lights. For an instant Jack thought about turning on a flashlight but immediately thought better of it. In a minute his eyes would get used to the dark. And besides, the light would make him an easy target.

The elevator lobby exited into north and south corridors. He turned right, toward the north-facing units. Ahead of him were six doors.

Pulling the Glock 17 from inside his coat, he was ready.

Behind the first door he found an unfinished machine room of unconnected pipes and loose wiring. The second door revealed a single large room, completely empty. The next three were equally abandoned.

That left only one door. *This must be it. There is too little time left for this to be wrong.*

Jack slowly pushed the door open and swept the room with his weapon.

Like the others it was completely empty.

This can't be right! They have to be here!

Jack stepped over to the large windows in the unit, looking for anywhere else Victor might be. As he turned to leave he pulled out his cell phone, but he stopped in the middle of dialing and froze. Jack's eyes were riveted to the entrance to the unit. Putting the phone back in his pocket, he slowly crept back to the door. The faintest of glows illuminated the hallway outside. *Where is that coming from?*

Jack crept into the hallway, his weapon at the ready. *There! It's a corner!* He saw it now. The corridor made a sharp turn to the left. In the dim light, without anything on the walls, Jack had thought that it was a dead end. Moving along the wall, Jack carefully rounded the corner.

He saw a man standing guard outside the last unit's door.

Gotcha.

"It's my father!" screamed Faina.

"I see him," answered Vaughn. "Can you see which part of the ballroom he's in?"

Faina didn't answer. She just stared at her father on the monitor.

"Faina!"

Her focus snapped to Vaughn as he asked her once more, "What part of the ballroom is he in?"

Faina looked at the camera number in the bottom

left corner. "That camera is . . . in the northeast corner of ballroom."

"Is there anything from the laptop?"

Faina intensely studied the small screen for a second. "No. Everything still is within acceptable parameters."

Vaughn's mind screamed. *We need more time!* "What happened to Sydney?"

"We lost her. I'm trying to jack us back in. I think—"

"Think!" Vaughn said.

"I've got it!" Faina said. "I'll get us back online."

Hang in there, Sydney.

"I see him," whispered Sydney in a slightly breathless voice.

"Where?" said Ivanna, peering at the stream of gentlemen.

"Over there." Sydney pointed out Anton Sorokin. Despite the tense look on his face, he did have a certain presence. Sydney noted traces of the confidence and security that she had seen in the photos of him in her file. Ivanna looked him over, a slightly puzzled look on her face.

"He is good-looking, but a little old."

Sydney made a show of checking her makeup with her compact mirror. "I prefer the term 'mature.'" Sydney put away her compact while covertly activating her PDA. "Besides, he's the head of the Dutch delegation. Wish me luck."

Sydney began to make her way steadfastly toward Sorokin, when all of a sudden the familiar sound of static buzzed in her ear. "Phoen**. This is **otgun. Targe* acq**red. Do you copy?"

Sydney whispered as inconspicuously as possible. "Shotgun, you're breaking up. Say again."

"We have acquired our target. Do you copy?"

"Affirmative. I'm approaching now and will await your go signal."

"Copy, Phoenix."

Sydney continued to move closer to Sorokin, who was standing near the fireplace studying something in his hand. *The blast could happen at any time!* Sydney noted that he didn't seem to be attempting to mingle or blend in. Sydney spoke as low as possible. "Outrigger, have you been monitoring?"

Sydney heard a sharp static *pop* meaning that Dixon had bitten down on his dental mic once, hard—the standard nonvocal affirmative signal.

"Copy. I'm moving into position from the east, but he doesn't know we're coming, so cover any possible escape routes to the north."

Here goes nothing. . . .

"We have Sorokin in sight, sir," stated one of Victor's men. "He's in position."

"Good," Victor replied, glancing at the photos on the wall. Four out of the five targets had been crossed out. "And our last guest?" His voice betrayed his growing frustration.

"We know he's there, sir. Zhursky's car dropped him in front of the hotel twenty-five minutes ago. We lost sight of him once he entered the hotel."

"Does he have rooms there?"

"No."

"Women?"

"Not that we know of."

"Victor," said his lieutenant, "we could detonate now. The blast should be more than sufficient . . ."

"No!"

The room went silent.

Victor very rarely raised his voice, and never to

his lieutenant. Instantly regretting the loss of control, he regained his composure and forced a smile.

"No, my friend. You're right. The blast will more than likely level the whole building."

Victor walked back to the window and looked out at the world he would soon redefine. The lieutenant watched as his employer stood at the glass, his face revealing nothing. Victor drew inward for strength; the artist is his own greatest well of motivation. When Victor finally did speak, it was as if to himself.

"But we must wait. . . . They all must be in the ballroom."

CHAPTER 16

Sydney was ten feet from Anton Sorokin when he turned and saw her. He was near a slightly raised stage where a quintet was tuning up to perform. What happened next caught her off guard.

He looked at her as though he *recognized* her!

Impossible, Sydney thought. *Perhaps Victor's men are behind me.* But as she moved closer it became obvious that Sorokin was, in fact, reacting to her. *But how?* One thing was clear; Sorokin was now definitely trying to get away from her.

"Why is my father fleeing?" Faina asked

urgently—almost accusingly—in Sydney's ear.

"I don't know!" Sydney said, meaning it.

Sydney couldn't deduce why Sorokin was purposefully keeping his distance from her. But if he was trying to avoid her why did he circle a relatively small area? If he moved into the main part of the hall it would have been easier to escape in the crowd.

And then Sydney understood. *This is the target area!*

She knew she had to get to Sorokin immediately, before the bomb was detonated. The lives of everyone in the room depended on it.

Sydney ignored the panicked voice in her head telling her that surely when Faina indicated that the bomb had been activated, she would be nowhere near close enough to stop the tragedy. *I'll never make it!*

And then her prayers were answered.

Sorokin didn't see Dixon until Dixon's hand was on his shoulder, and he whirled around in fear. His fingers tensed above the implanted detonator.

"Wait," Dixon commanded. When he nodded to Sydney, Sorokin turned pale.

"Please, let me go. . . . My daughter . . . ," Sorokin pleaded as Dixon maintained a firm grip on his arm.

The string quintet began playing, and the area directly in front of them filled with couples gracefully dancing to the music. Sydney had no choice but to take the long way around. Smiling and muttering apologies, she hurriedly made her way to Sorokin.

Please don't hear Faina's voice.

Less than four feet from her goal another voice spoke to her.

"Excuse me, but you are way too beautiful not to be enjoying this music," said a young man in a tuxedo. He was close enough for Sydney to smell several drinks on his breath. Smiling, Sydney tried to move around him, but he wouldn't be easily dismissed.

"Surely one dance won't be too much trouble?"

Sydney fought down the urge to take this obstacle out with a sharp thrust.

"Sorry, I don't think my husband would care for that," she said as she tried again to get around him. The drunk blocked her path. He lifted her left hand. Over her intoxicated suitor's shoulder, Sydney could see Dixon stalling Sorokin. She could almost touch him.

"Husband?" The man laughed. Holding up her hand, he said, "I see no ring."

Still not wanting to draw more attention to herself, Sydney gently but firmly pulled her hand away.

"Please, sir."

"Just one waltz. I promise that if you don't care for it, we'll only have one more."

Please, Faina, hold off a few more seconds. . . .

Sydney took the intoxicated man's arm and deliberately turned him directly into a passing waiter's path. The waiter spilled a full tray of champagne all over the drunk.

"You imbecile!"

The waiter apologized profusely even though he was not the one to blame. "I'm sorry, sir. Please let me assist you in the washroom."

Sydney used this distraction to cover the last four feet to Sorokin. It was not until she was right next to him that she could see how truly terrified he was of her. Perspiration coated his forehead, and his eyes were open wide. Gently she touched his sleeve. She felt a jolt of terror shake his body as he turned to face her.

"Zhursky! He's in the ballroom!"

Victor rushed over to the screen. There was intense silence as the men gathered around the monitor. Then one of them pointed to the bottom left corner of the screen.

"Over there. Near the bar, that is Emile Zhursky."

Victor allowed himself a tight smile. "Where's Sorokin? Prepare to detonate."

"Victor, you'd better take a look at this," his lieutenant called from his computer station.

"What is it?" Victor said.

The lieutenant pointed to his monitor. Sorokin was standing next to another tuxedoed man in front of a group of performing musicians. And then he saw what had alarmed the lieutenant. On the other side of Sorokin was a very attractive woman in an evening gown. It took him a moment to make the connection but then it hit him. . . . *It's the woman from the photograph!*

Victor's face was ashen. "Detonate the vest!" he shouted. "Do it now!"

CHAPTER 17

Dozens of couples waltzed around Sydney and Sorokin.

Sydney desperately tried to calm Sorokin, but he kept trying to back away. To blend in with the dancers, she sidled up close, one hand locked onto his and her other arm gripping him strongly from behind.

"Listen to me," Sydney said into his ear as soothingly as she could.

"Please . . . stay away from me!" Sorokin replied in an anguished hush. He trembled beneath her grip.

"Anton, I'm here to help you."

"You can't. No one can."

Sydney continued to dance with Sorokin. Gently, she tried to guide him toward the service exit at the far end of the dance floor, where she saw Dixon waiting.

Sorokin's eyes were wild. "You can't help. You don't know," he said.

"That they took your wife, your daughter . . ."

"My wife is dead!" he said emphatically.

"I know, and I'm sorry," Sydney said, "but your daughter, Faina, is safe. We rescued her from the mortuary."

"You're lying!"

"No. Why would I?"

"Because that's exactly what I'd tell me if I were you."

Sydney leaned into him, her mouth again to his ear. "Let me stop this."

Sorokin looked unsure, a desperate hope in his eyes. "You really have her? My daughter?"

"Faina is alive. In fact, she's right outside."

Suddenly Sorokin shook his head. "I don't believe you! I cannot afford to believe you."

"Anton, you can't afford not to."

* * *

Back inside the news truck, Vaughn's eyes darted from monitor to monitor. "Do you see anyone who could be one of Victor's men?" he asked Faina. *I can't believe it! We have Sorokin. Now Sydney just needs to disarm the explosives in time. . . .*

Faina didn't answer. Her eyes were riveted to her laptop. The moment she feared was happening right now. They found her father but the explosives' sensors had just been activated.

To her rising horror, everything checked out.

"Sydney!" she screamed. "It's happening. Do it now!"

Faina's scream was distorted by the tiny speaker in Sydney's ear. Dropping her left arm, Sydney retrieved the PDA from her handbag. She returned her hand to Sorokin's neck without missing a step in their waltz. Sliding the PDA onto the back of his neck, Sydney pushed the button. *Please work,* was the only thought that pulsed through her mind.

Sydney waited for the explosion. To her great relief, it never came.

Sydney looked into Sorokin's tense eyes, smiled, and exhaled. "We did it."

* * *

"I SAID DO IT!" Victor roared.

"We've tried, sir! The signal's been sent. Either they jammed it or they disabled the receiver somehow."

Despite his rage Victor stared mutely out the window. The rest of the room waited silently for his orders. Only after a tremendous effort was he able to regain his composure. He turned to his lieutenant. "Pack this up. Get the men out of here. . . ."

"But Victor—"

"Do it!" He stopped and took a breath. "If they know about Sorokin, they know about us!"

Victor walked over to the table lined with monitors and picked up a comms set. The remote detonation of the vest may have been foiled, but he had installed a backup measure—the switch glued to Anton Sorokin's palm.

"Anton, this is Victor," he relayed to Anton's hidden earpiece. "You will activate the switch in your hand, or I shudder to think what will happen to your daughter."

Sydney sensed something was wrong. They had been making progress toward the edge of the floor to meet Dixon and make their escape, when suddenly Sorokin stopped. His body fought her once again. Sydney squeezed his hand. "Sorokin?" But he didn't seem to hear her.

Sorokin broke out in a cold sweat; his eyes glancing at his left hand. Sydney followed his gaze and for the first time saw the camouflaged switch. Their eyes met.

"I'm sorry . . . ," Sorokin mumbled, his eyes filling with tears. He tried to pull his hand away, but Sydney's grip was like a vise.

Then Sydney saw the earpiece. *Victor is feeding him instructions!* It all made sense. Victor must be close by. "Listen to me," Sydney said. "Victor is a liar. I'm telling you the truth. I was with Faina less than an hour ago."

Over Sorokin's shoulder, Sydney caught sight of Dixon moving toward them. Sorokin again tried to free his hand.

Sydney was losing the battle to keep him calm.

"Your daughter is still alive. I can take you to her right now."

But Sorokin was listening to two voices and was torn, trying to guess who held the truth—the one whom he wanted to believe or the man who had already destroyed his life once.

Sydney's hand could just about reach the switch. "Look around," she said. "Are you going to be responsible for killing all these people? What would your wife have said?"

Sorokin began shaking, the horrors of the past twenty-four hours catching up to him. Too much pain had already been inflicted. He would add no more. Turning around and staring boldly at the windows, Sorokin said, almost to himself, "You're wrong about artists, Victor. No king is more powerful than the muse." He then surprised Sydney by reaching up and tearing the tiny receiver out of his ear.

"Take me to my daughter."

Jack slowly retreated around the corner, never taking his eyes off the sentry. The man was approximately seven meters away. Most likely Jack could take him out once his back was turned . . . but then he heard a noise. Peering around the corner, Jack saw the unit's door open and another man came out. Jack silently cursed. *One, maybe, but not two. Who knows how many more are inside?*

Peering around the corner again, Jack sighted another man, and now they all were busily packing equipment into the elevator. *They must have been compromised. Otherwise I would have heard the explosion next door.* Pulling his weapon, he discarded the silencer. *Accuracy's more important than stealth now.*

Rounding the corner, Jack opened fire on the men. Three of Victor's men went down. Other men streamed out of the unit and dove behind what little cover there was, returning fire. Jack, too, was forced to take cover.

Victor and his lieutenant were the only two left in the unit.

"See what's going on out there," Victor said.

Pulling his weapon, the lieutenant headed for the door. Victor looked down at the hotel. The lieutenant rushed back in. "We need to leave."

"Not yet," said Victor in a neutral voice. "I don't think he's going to do it. . . ."

"Three of our men are down. The authorities . . . ," said the lieutenant, concerned.

Victor, his plan no longer viable, steamed with rage.

"Please, Victor. Now is the time."

Tossing the microphone aside, Victor followed his lieutenant out.

Under the cover of gunfire he locked eyes for half a second with Jack Bristow. Most people were only muted tones in the background of his vision, but with Jack he saw a bold streak of red, a vibrant contrast to the gray tones in which he viewed most everyone else.

As quick as it was there, it was gone. His lieutenant yanked him into the elevator and clear of danger.

Jack was down to his last clip. Slamming it home, he pointed his Glock 17 down the corridor . . . at nothing! Cautiously Jack moved up to the apartment door. Empty. He ran for the elevator.

The atmosphere in APO was one of celebration. Marshall, Weiss, and Nadia were basking in their success when a message window appeared on Marshall's computer screen. He popped on his comms set and answered.

"This is Merlin."

"They're gone," Jack Bristow said plainly but with urgency in his voice.

"Who's gone?"

"Victor and the rest of the vests."

All of a sudden Marshall's full attention was on

his workstation. Nadia and Weiss stopped their joking and looked on.

"Okay, Raptor. I'm alerting our assets in the city. The airport and train stations will be saturated within thirty minutes."

"It's too late for that." Jack took the steps to the lobby four at a time. "Our target will already have a plan to get any extra explosive units out of the country quickly, probably by air."

By now Jack was at the door to the lobby and his voice dropped to a whisper.

"Merlin, you need to find out how he's doing it and try to delay him. Do you understand?"

"I'm on it."

"Contact me as soon as you do. Raptor out."

Faina's body pulsed with adrenaline. She had helped Sydney narrowly save a room full of people and, more important, her father.

"You did it, Faina. You saved him," said Vaughn, letting himself savor a few moments of relief.

"Thank you," Faina replied. But a new thought crept into her mind. "What happens next?"

"We get you and your father to safety," Vaughn said plainly.

This didn't satisfy the growing emotion in Faina. And that emotion was *rage.*

She was glad her father was safe. *But that isn't enough.* She looked at the laptop and began typing. Her hands flew furiously. So much so that Vaughn quit packing up their equipment and looked at the screen with concern.

"What is it?" he asked her.

"You'll see in a second," she replied, working rapidly.

Vaughn searched the screen, trying to understand the code that she was producing. Suddenly she stopped, exhaled, and hit the return key.

Faina tilted the laptop toward Vaughn. It flashed wildly and reflected its chaotic pattern on his face. Seconds later Vaughn's eyes rolled upward and he collapsed on the floor of the news truck.

Faina snatched up the laptop and prepared to leave. *It's not enough. I need to find Victor.*

"The one on the end," whispered Dixon as he, Sydney, and Sorokin made their way through the maze of news trailers behind the hotel.

Moments earlier Dixon had safely cut the wires to Sorokin's palm switch.

Sydney opened the door to the particular truck Marshall had indicated. Neither Vaughn nor Faina was there to greet them.

Sorokin tried to go in, but Sydney held him back. Motioning to Dixon they moved into the truck's control room.

At first glance the room was empty. Then Dixon spotted the bound television technician. As Sydney crouched down to examine the unconscious man's vital, a familiar pair of shoes caught her eye beneath the console.

Vaughn was sprawled, unmoving, on the floor.

CHAPTER 18

"If there was a more 'wow' word then, well, wow . . . I'd use it." Marshall stammered. "People who suffer from epilepsy are often affected by certain light patterns, which are also often used as crowd control devices. Patterns of flashing lights can have an adverse affect on the human body. It's called photosensitive epilepsy. "

"Or they can be used to knock out Vaughn," Sydney said, behind the wheel of a beat-up Mercedes 560 SEL, hot-wired from the valet parking lot. After reviving Vaughn, they discovered that

233

Faina had taken the Audi. "We need to know where Faina's going."

"What I need to know is how you allowed a teenager to render you unconscious," accused Sorokin. Vaughn didn't have an answer.

"You said she took the computer, right?" asked Marshall. "Well, if I were after the man who just killed my mom, and I knew the residual signal my jamming device gave off . . ."

"Marshall, can we do the same thing?" Sydney asked.

"I don't know what to look for. . . ."

"No, not the jamming signal—the laptop."

Even over the speaker Marshall sounded excited. "Right! If she's tracking him, she must be jacked into a wireless network."

"Find her."

Driving up in a Silver BMW M5, Dixon pulled up to the sidewalk outside the Oskarhurst Building and threw open the door for Jack.

"Get in. We've got a problem."

Moments later Dixon had told Jack of all that had happened next door at the hotel, including Faina's disappearance while on Vaughn's watch.

"How could he have been such an idiot?" Jack asked.

Dixon shrugged. "She is only a kid, Jack. . . ."

"Faina Sorokin is anything but just a kid. Is Marshall able to track her?"

Dixon nodded. "Yes. We've been tracking the wireless signal from Vaughn's laptop. Faina is tracking the vests, and Marshall and Nadia are tracking Faina." He pressed down on the accelerator as he swerved between two slower cars. "She's heading to Ruzyne International Airport."

"For revenge, she plans to detonate the vests."

"That is the general assumption," Dixon said as he noticed Jack pull out his Glock and check the clip.

"Under no circumstances can we let her detonate those vests," Jack said.

Downshifting, Dixon deftly maneuvered the M5 onto the exit marked PRG—RUZYNE.

Vaughn was anything but happy. Being deceived by a seventeen-year-old girl was humiliating. He noted Sorokin glaring at him from the backseat; it wasn't exactly congratulatory.

Sydney's thoughts were elsewhere. *Why didn't*

I read the signs better? How could I miss her quest for vengeance?

Her thoughts were interrupted by Sorokin's panicked words. "I can't lose my daughter."

"Don't worry," said Sydney. "We'll get her."

I have to find Faina.

Vaughn picked up on Sydney's distraction. He saw, as he uncannily did in so many instances, exactly what was going through Sydney's mind. This was the woman he loved.

"We'll find her," Vaughn said, like a small, needed squeeze of the hand.

Time seemed to be moving at double speed. Sydney hardly believed the green digital display numbers on the radio that said only seven minutes had passed since they had left for the airport. Moments later the sedan was rolling past the welcome sign to Ruzyne International Airport. Sydney's slight relief at their arrival was obliterated when Marshall informed them, "I have bad news and worse news. Faina's signal ended at the airport. With all the various transmissions going through the property, there's virtually no way that I'll be able to find her."

Then Weiss chimed in with new information.

"Airline tickets in the name of one of Victor's aliases have been confirmed. Five seats were purchased for an international flight to Barcelona. They had no luggage checked. The vests must be carry-on."

"That's not good," said Vaughn, thinking of the hundreds of innocent passengers on board.

"Flight nine twenty-two is scheduled to depart from the gate in twenty minutes," Weiss reported. Vaughn asked flatly, "Runway?"

"Nine twenty-two has not been given clearance for either runway, but—"

Marshall interrupted, "They're running an east and north take-off pattern. Favoring the north."

"In order to keep her laptop in a line of sight with the vests, she's probably at the perimeter," Sydney said. "I'm getting out here and I'll double back to it."

Vaughn protested as Sydney slammed on the brakes and the car skidded to a stop near a service entrance. As she climbed out of the car Vaughn yelled, "I'll go with—"

But she cut him off before he had a chance to finish. "Head to the east runway, with Sorokin. One of us will reach her."

And she was gone.

Vaughn knew there was no time left for arguing. He slid behind the wheel and punched the gas.

"I already checked, Jack." The tone in Marshall's voice confirmed that he had verified more then once. Those who had ever encountered the work relationship between Jack Bristow and Agent Flinkman knew that Marshall was deathly afraid of Sydney's father. Jack was an intelligent man and respected Marshall greatly for the talents that he brought to the team. That being said, it took a great deal of self-control, in Jack's opinion, for him not to lash out at Marshall in response to his inane blathering about everything but what was on topic. Marshall had learned to try and curb this personality trait and double-check all facts in tense conflicts with Mr. Bristow.

Before any further advances could be made, Marshall explained, "It would take me too long to get in the system to get you a ticket on the plane. I'm sorry, but you'll have to find an alternative plan to—"

"Thank you, switching to comms."

Dixon threw his car in park at the airport's white zone. He and Jack were out of the car almost before it stopped moving. No more than a few travelers noticed them. As in most airports, people were too wrapped up in their own worlds to care about two men leaving a car at the curb.

Five seconds later Dixon was headed toward the perimeter gate of the east runway. He worried about whether they would be able to stop the girl before Jack—or he himself—had to shoot her. This was a desperate situation, and he hoped that he wouldn't have to make a desperate decision.

Jack and Dixon moved through the service area of the airport. The corridor was painted a dull brown. A sharp contrast, no doubt, to the bright, sleek white-and-silver design of the main international terminal. While the general public was offered such amenities as kiosks selling overpriced bestselling paperback novels and a Starbucks every hundred feet, the behind-the-scenes arteries of the airport were another world.

A silent nod between Jack and Dixon was the signal to mutually open tiny black leather cases containing an array of falsified identification cards. "Flinkman's specialties" were what Dixon called them. They were the best damn fakes anyone could get their hands on.

Jack flipped past one identification certificate that claimed he was a police officer. That falsification he typically used only as a last resort. Showing it, Jack knew, would mean phone calls to supervisors and filling out paperwork. No one wanted that: People, he had learned, liked to negotiate situations in ways that hassled them the least. With this in mind, Jack made his selection and displayed a personal favorite backdoor key ID card. Dixon approved and found the corresponding card that sold them both as Federal Express representatives.

Turning a corner, Jack saw a small workers' break room off to the right. The room was the same dismal color scheme as the rest of the interior halls and currently free of any personnel. With a nod, Dixon followed Jack into the break room.

The smell of reheated frozen dinners hung in the air. A television was mounted high in one corner. It was set to the Russian MTV channel, and although there was no sound, closed-captioning scrolled across the bottom of the screen.

Jack scanned the room quickly. There were vending machines with candy and cold sandwiches along the wall. The trash can was overfilled. Dixon had already found one of those seventy-two-ounce

Styrofoam drink cups to use. Jack tossed a coin of local currency to Dixon, and he selected a soda.

With a knowing nod from the gray-haired agent, they both knew that getting through should be no problem.

Victor smirked as his ticket was scanned at the boarding gate. He'd had some reservations about walking through the metal detectors earlier, but pushed them away recalling that he himself had seen Sorokin do it an hour earlier.

Now, moving down the narrow corridor toward the plane, he could see his other mules entering ahead of him. The muted noise of jets arriving and leaving pumped familiarly through the boarding hall. Everything seemed normal, everything except for the pained itch of failure that Victor felt. Trying to calm the ache, he muttered to himself, "At least I've gotten away."

As Victor sat in his first-class seat waiting for the flight to take him to safety, he reviewed the disappointing turn of events. Killing the wife was the first mistake. It had made handling Sorokin much more difficult. And Sorokin was to blame also, he decided, for not understanding that he'd been beaten. Or maybe the girl, for having the audacity to escape, erasing his leverage against her father. Well, none of it mattered anymore, anyway. The project had failed and he was on his way out.

But not without its silver lining. He would more than recoup his losses in the coming months by selling the remaining stealth technology he'd acquired from that painfully annoying little girl. Still, nothing would have sold his promises better than the results of Sorokin's demise with worldwide news coverage. All these things fretted him greatly as he forced another smile at the uniformed flight attendant offering welcomes and seat information at the entrance of the aircraft.

This will be over soon, he thought, still seething about the events of the night. His face showed nothing of his anger, an old KGB trick that he had mastered to blend in. He was utterly forgettable. He projected that image when undercover, and it had not failed him for the length of both his legitimate and his criminal careers. It had been fourteen years since any job he had taken was not completed. A great record, but even professional golfers go out of their minds when they miss a three-foot putt at the end of a great round. For now though, he would try and think of better things than the itch of the explosive-laden Kevlar vest that fit him a little too snugly.

Sydney searched frantically. There were large storage crates scattered almost mazelike around the edge of the airfield. She had reached for her sidearm out of habit. This struck her as odd, since Faina was unarmed, at least in the sense of bullets and a gun. But Sydney realized that Faina was in fact much more dangerous than the average thug.

In her training at SD-6 and the CIA, Sydney had mastered how to seize control of an opponent's weapon. She'd committed to memory the differences in approach one should take depending on whether an enemy was armed with a handgun or a machine gun or a shotgun. She was a master at all the various techniques. Bullets and steel were one thing, but Faina posed a greater threat to Sydney. *A keen mind is much more difficult to disarm.*

Sydney thought of the speech that Anna Sorokin had given Faina regarding decisions. Would Faina use the heart, mind, or fist to enact what she considered justice? More important, Sydney found herself at a loss for which method to use against her.

* * *

"Just a sec more," was Marshall's response to Jack's question. In less than the estimated time, Marshall responded. "Load platform two."

"Thank you," Jack said cooly as he and Dixon rounded the corner. They found a small security checkpoint set up in front of the grand chaos of the shipping and receiving area. Much of the mail going to and from Prague filtered through this international hub. But with budgets and bottom lines always at the core of things, the checkpoint was modest. It had a similar setup as the security stations that separated the boarding gates from the ticket area; a stand-alone metal detector blocked two thirds of the hallway, and a small table, used as a desk, covered the remaining space.

A short, stocky man in an airport security uniform stood up as they approached. He had a thick bushy mustache, and the rest of his face was peppered with three-day-old black stubble. His bored gaze had the look of a man that didn't care much about much, simply a slave to the inadequate paycheck that came to him on a regular basis.

"Identification, please," the man said.

Jack took a sip through the straw in the large

drink cup Dixon had procured from the small workers' break room. He smiled and quipped about seeing the end of the soccer match that was on earlier.
Jack then set the drink down on the table along with
his wallet, change, and watch. Dixon did the same
with his personal items as the guard grumbled, "I
lost fifty on that stupid game."

The guard grabbed Jack's and Dixon's personal
items and then slid them around to the other side
of the metal detector.

As Jack walked through the metal detector,
Dixon added his opinion. "I lost too. My third week
in a row." The guard shook his head sympatheti-
cally.

Jack and Dixon pocketed their personal effects,
and then Jack reached around the detector for his
cup and took another sip. "Have a good night,"
Jack said as he walked off.

The guard waved farewell.

Dixon smiled internally. How *normal* Jack
Bristow could become when he needed to be! Five
feet past the guard, Dixon watched as Jack subtly
morphed back into the thick-skinned person he
was used to seeing.

Ducking into the nearest restroom just inside

the vast packaging room of the airport shipping warehouse, both agents moved with purpose. Dixon braced the door as Jack set his cup on the counter. Popping the lid, he retrieved two standard-issue semiautomatic handguns and several backup clips, which had been wedged tightly inside the cup. Once the guns had been removed, Jack discarded the closeable sandwich bag that Dixon had poured soda into and sealed with the straw in it.

Jack tossed Dixon his weapon and clips and quickly reassembled his gun. Noting that a bullet was in the chamber, they left the restroom, knowing only the least of their worries were behind them.

Damn it! Where is she?

The ground before Sydney was a powdery brown dust. When she moved across it, she kicked up little dirt clouds. As much as it bothered her lungs, its texture did produce one great bit of usefulness: footprints.

She saw them on the ground everywhere in various sizes and shapes. She compared her own foot with two track possibilities. Faina was significantly shorter than Sydney, not having hit her final growth spurt yet, which aided in finding a clue to which way she might have gone.

The first print was about the correct dimensions, but upon further inspection she dismissed it. The footstep's features were of a work boot. Sydney could tell from the imprints it left in the ground that the heel was raised, and she recalled that Faina was wearing sneakers.

The second print was a stronger possibility. Part of the design of the sole's logo was visible. Faina's shoes were old, but not so worn that the underside grooves would be rubbed away. Sydney measured the imprint with her own foot, then guessed a young girl's stride. It had to be her. She immediately sprang into motion, following the footprints.

Pressing through the maze of shipping crates, Sydney made a sharp right and found herself at a chain-link fence. On just the other side of it, more shipping containers blocked the view of the runway. The trail went cold.

Just then a plane rumbled overhead, reminding Sydney again what was at stake, as well as the ever-closing window in which she had to operate.

Where the hell did she go?

Turning, Agent Bristow saw in the darkness

that the shipping container closest to her had small rungs built into its side. Sydney grabbed hold of a rung above her and ascended to the top of the large metal box.

Once on top of the container, she peered into the night and down toward the lights of the airfield. In the distance, squarely positioned in the shadows, Sydney found Faina. The young woman was seated with her legs crossed, and Sydney could make out the light blue glow of a laptop computer screen. Faina was in a perfect position to take down a northbound aircraft.

Immediately Sydney checked her PDA, but as she feared, it was dead. Marshall had told her that it would have only enough juice in it for one pulse. Realizing that her pulse weapon was useless, she unlocked the safety on her Glock. She didn't want to harm Faina. On the other hand, there was no way she could let her obliterate an international flight full of innocent lives.

With great regret, she approached Faina.

CHAPTER 19

The dark blue service jacket that Dixon wore was coarse, and a fair bit too small; it didn't help that his work shirt underneath was at least a size too big. His hat was stained and ill-fitting, but when he tried to adjust it, he found that the tightening strap had been replaced with duct tape.

With a sigh, Dixon looked at himself in the small rearview mirror of the forklift he was about to operate. An industrial bulb on the worn yellow painted control board before him glowed to life as he turned the ignition key. He released the clutch and used the forklift to transport a large Federal Express cargo box.

In ten seconds he was out of the hangar and headed toward the aircraft.

Before him was a DC10 pulling away from the airport hub. And just beyond that was a 767— flight 922. Dixon pulled up to it just before the side hatch was sealed.

"One more," Dixon yelled into the chilly night.

The man working the jet's cargo door made a slight fuss, but ultimately allowed Dixon to load one last crate.

Inside flight 922's cargo bay, the static noise of the airfield outside was muffled. In a few seconds the drone of the engines was all that could be heard. If there was anyone to listen, they would have heard a *click.* It wasn't a shift in luggage, but rather the distinctive flick of a flashlight switch.

Half a second later, a small circular beam glowed from behind the thick plastic Fed Ex cover of the container that Dixon had loaded into the hull of the jumbo jet. A knife blade punctured the covering and sliced a four-foot slit down to the base of the unit. The sides peeled back to reveal the grand entrance of Agent Jack Bristow.

"Mr. Stoliski, another glass of champagne?" asked the long-legged blonde in a flight attendant uniform. She was slim, sexy, but had the distinctive appearance of someone merely going through the motions of her job. The passenger nodded, exchanging his empty glass for another complimentary golden bubbly.

As the attendant moved down the aisle, Victor thought to himself about the time when he'd killed the *real* Mr. Stoliski. Victor was still in the KGB, and Stoliski was a traitor to the Communist state. His murder wasn't sanctioned, but Victor and some of his closely tied affiliates had their own beliefs about the benefit of the troublemaker's death. Stoliski had been one of his first murders and was thus nostalgically his favorite alias.

Victor Pushov reclined in his soft leather seat. The seat next to him was empty, and with the takeoff just minutes away it looked as if he would have plenty of elbow room for his flight.

Airline attendants flitted about, offering hot towels. Victor took his without even looking up. His attention was on his drink. Through the glass of champagne a shadow appeared, darkening his light yellow bubbled beverage. *It appears I'll have a neighbor after all.*

Victor made no attempt to even acknowledge the man's presence. He hated polite small talk. But to the flight attendants, people were paying customers. And those in first class had a reputation for demanding everything coming to them.

The blond flight attendant leaned across Victor with a small terry cloth gripped in a set of tongs. The late arriver reached over to receive the towel and responded with an even-metered thank-you.

Only then did Victor recognize the person sitting next to him.

"Hello," was all Jack Bristow had to say to freeze Victor's blood.

Sydney slowly approached Faina.

If I frighten her, she might blow up the plane.

For the most part, her advance was masked by the sound of large jet engines.

As Sydney edged nearer she hoped that she could simply separate Faina from the computer.

She did not want to battle this girl, who had already suffered so much.

Sydney was just ten feet away when Faina spoke. She didn't turn around. Her focus was still very much on monitoring the signals resonating on the laptop.

"I figured you'd show up," Faina said casually. Her tone was confident, which instantly worried Sydney.

As Sydney had already perceived, the mind was far more difficult to disarm than a gun. If Faina had a Glock, she'd have at best seventeen rounds. The mind, on the other hand, could be continually reloaded for battle.

"You're a smart girl, Faina," Sydney replied, letting the truth hang in the air. Faina's attention remained focused on her computer. Sydney narrowed her hazel eyes as she continued with the rest of her thought. "That's why I don't understand why you're doing this."

Sydney took a step closer but stopped at Faina's next words. "I have Agent Vaughn's weapon, Ms. Bristow. Please don't come any closer." The evenness of Faina's voice was more frightening than the threat.

How do I reach her . . . ?

Pondering the best move, Sydney's rational calm came to a screeching halt when her comms delivered more dire news. Marcus Dixon said, "Sydney, your father is on the plane."

Vaughn's voice interjected. "Maybe I can—"

"Flight nine twenty-two, has already pulled away from the gate."

Sydney's nervous system was infused with adrenaline. She gave herself five seconds to be scared and then found the icy calm that her father portrayed so well.

"Your mother asked you to make choices based on the mind. Faina, do you think that this choice isn't of the heart or the fist?"

A teardrop slid down Faina's cheek. She clutched her mother's necklace against her chest.

"You have a choice here to do what's right," said Sydney.

"I don't want—"

Sydney interrupted her. "You asked me about my failures, and I told you the truth. Agents can make mistakes. It's a reality I have to accept. But to willingly murder innocents . . . I couldn't live with myself if I caused that. I don't think anyone could.

Even you, Faina. This act will haunt you. This action will become your life. It'll never be the same—"

"It'll never be the same now!" Faina protested. "My mother was taken away."

"People who choose to hurt others change," Sydney said. "They choose a new direction to take their life, and the people who love them don't go on that journey. They get left behind."

Sydney paused briefly to let that information sink in.

"Your father, he loves you, Faina. I looked in his eyes, and he was going to kill a room full of people on the dying wish that you would have a life. You will take that wish away from him if you do this."

Faina began typing slowly on the laptop. Sydney hoped that her words were getting through to her. She contemplated drawing her weapon.

"Revenge always comes from the heart and the fist. Make the decision that your mother would want you to make," Sydney said.

Faina typed a few more keystrokes. Her cheeks were streaked with tears. She was beginning to tremble. When she finally spoke, her voice was loaded with questioning and regret.

"I'm sorry, but I have to go through with this."

CHAPTER 20

The entire crew at APO was absolutely silent as they monitored the airport. Marshall had piped the air traffic control tower audio into his office. As the tower cleared flight 922 for takeoff, Weiss noticed that the bagel in his hand had been in the same position for the past twenty minutes. He set it down on the counter as the pilot acknowledged the clearance and began the roll out to the north runway.

"I took you for a first-class traveler, Mr. Pushov," Jack said with eyes that promised to kill Victor if he moved. "My government tends to send me coach."

The two men looked at each other as the rolling plane came to a stop. Over the loudspeaker, the captain said, "We're third in line to take off on our nonstop to Barcelona. . . ."

The rest of it seemed to drone on. Jack also continued, "Believe it or not, I'm here to save you."

Victor didn't believe him. "You'll have to forgive me, but I doubt that is the case."

Jack gave Victor exactly one second to feel as if he had any control over the situation. "I understand you're quite the art aficionado. If you wish not to end up looking like a Jackson Pollock painting, I suggest you come with me."

Victor's eyes narrowed. His lips pursed, ready to speak, when he heard a distinctive, terrifying *beep* that stopped his heart. Jack confirmed the fear for him. "That small sound was in fact the sound of the explosive vest you're wearing arming itself."

Victor's eyes and every muscle in his face lost authority. In fact, they registered a thousand questions.

"Faina Sorokin has gone rogue," Jack said. "She knows you're on this flight, and she doesn't care how many people die as long as the red mist you'll leave behind is part of the rubble." Jack couldn't resist making him suffer. "This is what it's like to be the painting, not the artist."

Just then the captain's voice came over the loudspeaker again to inform the passengers that only one more plane remained ahead of them on the runway.

Jack was ice.

Victor began to sweat, the urgency of an instant decision overwhelming him.

"Now," Jack said quietly to his adversary, "would you like to talk about how we can help each other?"

Sydney raised her weapon.

She had prayed this moment wouldn't come, but now it seemed unavoidable.

The gun felt uncomfortable in her hands. Heavy, not in weight but with burden. She didn't want to even entertain the thought of what she might have to do.

"My father is on that plane. My father can get Victor Pushov off that flight, and we can punish him," Sydney said. "Victor Pushov will pay for everything he's done to you and everyone else he's ever hurt."

Faina continued to cry as she picked up Vaughn's gun. Her hand was noticeably shaky. It appeared as if this was the first time young Sorokin had ever held a weapon.

In her ear Sydney heard the voices of APO. She felt as helpless as Anton Sorokin must have only half an hour before. Marshall informed her that the last plane had just begun its takeoff. They had only seconds before flight 922 would be in the air.

"You won't shoot me, Agent Bristow. Not if you believe all the things you've been telling me." Faina looked at her, daring her to debate.

Sydney forced her next thought out. "No, Faina, killing you will turn me into exactly what we've been talking about. But I'll be able to say I saved four hundred lives, instead of murdering them and spreading the pain you feel to all of their families."

Faina used the barrel of Vaughn's gun to help herself stand up. This made Sydney nervous. The mental weapon was melding with the physical one. In reaction to Faina's move Sydney took two steps back and readied to fire if need be.

"I'm so lost. I'm so confused," Faina cried as the gun now swayed in her hand.

Sydney focused as best as she could.

Something has to happen.

Sydney spoke to Faina. She spoke to Vaughn. She even spoke to herself as she explained things to the girl before her. "Everybody gets lost. Smart people let themselves get found."

Faina's grip on her gun tightened. But instead of aiming at Sydney, she surprised them both by turning to the laptop and squeezing the trigger repeatedly. Each bullet was a release of pain.

Exhausted, Faina let the gun drop. She fell to her knees as if her legs could no longer support her. Sydney rushed toward Faina and enveloped the girl in her arms.

CHAPTER 21

It's quiet, thought Nadia as she completed her report about the Prague mission. Looking around the room, the few agents remaining were, like her, finishing paperwork or filing their reports before going home. But the fact of the matter was, Nadia really didn't need to be there at all. The paperwork she was doing could easily have been turned in the next day. In fact, it wasn't expected before late afternoon. But she had made a decision, and it was going to happen before she left.

And then it happened. The lights in Sloane's

office went out, turning the white wall into a muted gray. Looking up from her work, Nadia watched as his door slid shut. His back was to her, but when he turned to head out, she dropped her head to hide that she had been watching him.

Scanning the room, she watched him walk toward the elevator. She had wondered if he would stop by and see her, but then again, she had made it abundantly clear that their relationship was strictly professional.

Picking up her files, she headed over to cut him off. She moved agilely, weaving between desks and chairs. *This probably isn't the move I should be making, but I've got to say something.*

She caught him just after he pushed the button for the elevator. He stood before the metal doors, waiting.

He must have felt her approach—an old spy habit, perhaps—because he turned to greet her. As she was lost in her own thoughts, his gesture actually caught her off guard.

After a beat Nadia stepped closer to him. Sloane's face, as usual, betrayed nothing.

At first they shared an awkward silence. APO was most quiet at this hour, and speaking in such a quiet space seemed daunting to both of them. And honestly, neither one knew what to say.

Sloane looked at his daughter, wanting to speak but also knowing that this was a very fragile moment and that if there was going to be any chance of success, he would have to let her make her own play. So he patiently waited.

"I finished my report," Nadia said. Her voice was all business. Inside she cringed. *That was smooth. Why didn't you just leave a note on his desk?*

Sloane looked down at the file clutched in Nadia's hand. "Could you hold that until the morning? I was just on my way out."

"Of course, I should have thought first."

Sloane smiled.

"Tomorrow."

The doors to the elevator parted, but neither Sloane nor Nadia moved. Nadia couldn't even look at him. As the doors began to close Sloane stopped them with his briefcase. With a final glance at Nadia, he entered the waiting elevator. Still holding the door with his hand, he set down his briefcase. He was giving her every opportunity to open up to him. But with the subtlest look of defeat in her eyes, Nadia turned to go.

"Nadia?" Sloane's voice stopped her in her tracks. "I was thinking about what you said earlier, and . . ."

It's too late now, Nadia thought. Closing her eyes, she just decided to say it. "I don't think going out to dinner is a very good idea."

Sloane's face remained neutral but for an instant Nadia saw the faintest hint of true disappointment in his eyes. She saw his hand about to fall away to allow the elevator door to slide shut.

"I mean, really, I do not think there is anywhere in this city to get decent Argentine food," she said.

For a moment their eyes met. Both father and daughter looked for something, although neither one could have said quite what.

Nadia's next sentence began almost cautiously. "So why don't you come to my place, and I'll cook you a real Argentine dinner."

Finding it increasingly more difficult to keep his face neutral, Sloane's eyes began to shine. "That would be nice."

"Okay. How about on Sunday?"

"All right," he said. He dropped his hand to release the doors, then stopped them again. As they reopened he leaned out of the elevator. "Nadia?"

Nadia turned, her look showing her worry that he would want to back out this time.

"What kind of wine does one bring to an authentic Argentine dinner?"

Nadia's face broke into a beautiful smile. "Malbec, an Achaval Ferrer Finca Altamira. I hear ninety-nine is a good year."

Sloane smiled back tentatively. "Then I'll see you on Sunday."

Stepping back, he let the doors close. Nadia turned back to her desk, surprised to feel the smile still on her face.

The Falcon 10 private jet slipped effortlessly through the night sky on its way back to the United States.

In the passenger compartment, Dixon and Jack compiled their preliminary debrief on a laptop, speaking in hushed tones. Jack looked up from his paperwork at Dixon. "Didn't realize you were so adept with a forklift."

Dixon laughed, mainly because the night had been long and he needed to. He responded, "I knew that Class D license would come in handy one day." Dixon then motioned toward the photo of Victor Pushov in Jack's lap. "My comms unit failed. How did you convince him to get off the plane peacefully?"

Dixon could sense Jack's elation from the success of his plan, and he felt good to see him slightly at ease. Jack spoke low, as if he were giving away secrets.

"The lunch cooler from the mail room I took with me . . ."

Dixon nodded, remembering that Jack had grabbed a small cold storage container before being sealed into the shipping unit.

Jack continued, "I told the flight attendant that we were a team of doctors. I had a liver in the cooler for the prime minister's wife in Spain. I imparted that I had just learned that she had been moved from Barcelona to Rome and that myself and my team of surgeons needed to get off the plane."

"That accounts for the departure, but why would he leave?"

"I told him the truth," said Jack. Dixon noted how much Jack's phrasing just then sounded like Arvin Sloane's. "Faina was planning to blow the plane up the second it took off. I could only take the vests off him and his men if he disembarked the plane. And I promised to plea-bargain his case for a bigger fish. He'd serve no time."

"So they got off the plane and all ended well."

"And when I put the handcuffs on him, I smiled and let him know that art might always be truthful, but that I myself was not."

Dixon smiled at Jack playing Pushov. He attempted to talk more, but Agent Bristow had already begun going over his paperwork again. His moment of openness over, the protector knight in his unchanging suit of armor once again closed off the rest of world.

In the rear compartment of the aircraft, Vaughn tried in vain to sleep. Despite Faina's assertions to the contrary, he still felt the aftereffects of her stunt with the laptop. Marshall suggested that his ailments could last for as long as three days. Vaughn's initial feeling was anger, but he was well aware of how regretful Faina felt about her stunt. He decided to just try and get some sleep.

But none off that mattered to Sydney just then. She sat alone in the center of the rear compartment, her finished report in the laptop on the seat next to her, along with the crossword from the *Lidove Noviny* newspaper, also finished, and in Czech. What did matter to Sydney was where she was going now, not physically, but in her life. Seeing how Vaughn had changed was more than a little unnerving and threw her hopes for the future in doubt. The past year was life altering to say the least. But only now did she realize how much Vaughn . . . and *she* . . . had changed. When she and Vaughn were at her house— *How long ago was that? It seems like forever now—* she had felt for the first time in more than three years what it meant to be home. She had assumed that it was because Vaughn was there with her, but now she wasn't so sure. It had been so hard, watching him with Lauren. But now Lauren wasn't a physical threat any longer. She was gone. But there was still no denying that she had left her mark on Michael . . . and her.

Maybe that was it. It wasn't just that Vaughn was there with me, but the fact that Lauren wasn't. In a weird way, with Lauren's passing Sydney found herself free. Not in the petty "now Vaughn is all mine" sort of free, but rather, in knowing that that malevolent being was out of *her* life, she was able to unclench emotionally. Things that were always taut with stress felt a little more relaxed now.

But what about Vaughn?

This was a much more complex question, and one that she knew she would not be able to answer any time soon. *Do I love him? Yes.* Without a question she loved him. *But is it in the same way as before?* Another question she couldn't answer yet. So Sydney sat there thinking about where that left her. She was at the same time emotionally free and without direction, and it drained her.

It was then that a small flying object drove her out of her thoughts. Whatever it was hit the seat in front of her and fell to her feet. She reached down and felt around with her fingers until she found the small cardboard box. Pulling it up, she couldn't help but smile. It was a small box printed in the primitive two-color graphics only seen in the third world and old eastern-bloc countries. Even if she couldn't read the words on the box (and she could), she would have known what it was. The drawing on the front said it all. It was the kind of thing one would pick up at an airport or bus depot at the beginning of a long trip. It was a travel Scrabble game . . . in Czech!

Later, she thought. For now, Sydney decided

that it was good enough to enjoy the moment. Reality would come soon enough.

Without looking behind her, she asked Michael Vaughn, "Does this mean that we have to play in Czech?"

Christopher Hollier and R. P. Gaborno are both writers assistants for the *Alias* television series. They wrote the episode "Facade" for season three. They live in Burbank, California. This is their first book.

FULL DISCLOSURE

- **Exclusive interviews with the show's stars!**
- **All the latest series news!**
- **Behind-the-scenes secrets!**
- **Fantastic pin-ups!**

Find out all you need to know in *Alias Magazine*

WATCH
ALIAS ON
abc

www.titanmagazines.com/us